Both brothers made much of Julia, flirting with her in a half serious, half satirical manner. Harriet looked from Verney to Sir Richard, aware that something was happening which she could not understand. During the dance Verney talked to her quite a bit, but when the music was over he returned her to her seat, made a slight bow, and walked away.

When she saw Verney escorting Julia to supper, it was more than she could bear. Nearly crying with humiliation and disappointment, she did not know where to hide, until she was rescued by Louisa Capel, who had seen it all.

"Is he—do you think Verney is falling in love with Miss Johnson?" Harriet asked her.

"My dear child, Verney has never been in love in his life. He merely amuses himself with any female who takes his fancy."

All Harriet's hopes were finally dashed. She had come to the ball thinking Verney loved her—but if he never had, if she was simply one of his flirtations, it was only too natural that he should abandon her for the fascinating Julia. . . .

No Hint of Scandal

SHEILA BISHOP

ace books
A Division of Charter Communications Inc.
A GROSSET & DUNLAP COMPANY
51 Madison Avenue
New York, New York 10010

An ACE Book

Published simultaneously in Canada

2 4 6 8 0 9 7 5 3 1
Manufactured in the United States of America

Contents

PART ONE

Country Neighbours

1

WARDLEY PARSONAGE stood just inside the enclosed park that surrounded Wardley Hall, ensconced between the Dower House and the Church. The view from the breakfast parlour held nothing of the picturesque flavour for which Wardley was famous—not a vaulted arch or a leaping torrent in sight—but the Reverend Theo Capel, gazing out of the window on an April morning in the year 1811, was quite content with what he saw: green grass and a walnut tree, and the drive running down to the imposing gateway with its trim stone lodge.

"I wish you will come and eat your breakfast, my love," said his wife from the table behind him.

He turned, and came to join her: a powerfully-built man of thirty-three, with a good open face and the look of someone who was used to being out in all weathers; he had already been walking about the parish for the first two hours of the day, while she was attending to the housekeeping and visiting the nursery. They observed each other comfortably across the white, starched cloth.

Louisa Capel was small and pretty. Her eyes were blue and her fair hair was thick and glossy under her cap. She had a great deal of assurance, for she was not merely the Rector's wife but also, through a variety of circumstances, the lady of greatest consequence in the parish, accustomed to managing the lives of most of the other inhabitants, including her husband.

She was annoyed to hear a brisk rap on the front door, followed by sounds of movements in the hall.

"Who can that be, at this hour? What is Hatton about, to let them in? Tiresome creatures, they never leave you in peace."

The parlour door had opened a fraction, and an amused voice said: "How fierce you sound, Louisa. Shall I go away again?"

"Oh, it's you, my dear fellow," exclaimed the Rector. "Have you come to breakfast?"

"I haven't been invited yet," said his elder brother, strolling in without ceremony, "and I dare not hope that Louisa will take pity on me, she disapproves of encroaching parishioners so early in the day."

"How can you be so foolish?" said Louisa, smiling and ringing the bell. "We have not seen you since Monday; sit down and tell us your news. (Fetch a cup and saucer for Sir Richard, if you please, Hatton.)"

Sir Richard Capel took the chair beside her. He was taller than his brother and extremely handsome, with raven-black hair and a splendid profile. As a young man he had been a perfect Adonis, and at thirty-seven, after the tragedy of his wife's long illness and death, there was an added distinction of character and resolution written in his face. He was the eighth holder of the baronetcy that dated back to the Civil War, a Member of Parliament and pa-

8

tron of the living he had presented nine years ago to Theo.

Now that he was alone at the Hall with his children, he relied a good deal on the companionship of his brother and sister-in-law.

"You asked for my news," he said, stirring his coffee. "I have two items for you. First of all, Verney is on the wing. We may expect him here for dinner."

Theo looked up quickly. "Why do you suppose he is coming?"

"I imagine he is very short of money. I hope you don't feel obliged to tell me that I ought not to receive him. He is a prodigal, after all—and I'm sure he doesn't enjoy eating husks."

"I never presume to teach you morality, Richard," said the Rector, rather flushed. "You ought to know that by this time."

"Yes, I ought. I beg your pardon."

"Well, I call it outrageous," declared Louisa, "and exactly like Verney's effrontery. It's all very well to speak of prodigals—has he shown the smallest sign of repentance?"

"No," said Richard coolly. "He never could say he was sorry as a child. Give him his due, Louisa. Wardley is still his home, and he has no other since he had to leave the regiment."

"He could have exchanged. He wasn't obliged to sell out."

"I don't think the Army suited him."

The fact was that his youngest brother, serving with the Guards in and around London, had committed almost every folly available to a junior officer in a smart regiment with nothing to do but amuse himself, and had finally broken an unwrit-

9

ten law by seducing the wife of one of his brother officers.

All young men were entitled to sow a few wild oats, but this was something different and very disgraceful. Louisa had no sympathy with Verney, and did not much want to meet him at present. No hint of scandal had cast a shadow over the Capel family for at least three generations. (In less enlightened ages their ancestors had of course behaved just as badly as everyone else, though always in an aristocratic way.) Louisa thought it would have been far better for Verney to go on soldiering in some other part of England, or even in Spain, until the memory of his latest exploit had been decently blurred; she was just about to say so when Theo changed the subject.

"What was your second piece of news, Richard?"

"Something very much to the point. Bowyer has found a new tenant to take his place at Bell Cottage."

"A new tenant? Surely that wasn't laid down in his lease?"

"Certainly not. But it seems that while he was in London, getting ready to sail for the West Indies, he met some old friends of his mother's who are anxious to settle in this part of the country—a maiden lady and her companion. They are negotiating the terms with Coverdale."

"How odd," commented Louisa, "to choose a house and a situation they have never seen."

"Miss Johnson comes from the north, and has been advised to try a milder climate. I believe they are anxious to be settled."

"I dare say they will make useful neighbours," said the Rector. "Perhaps they will help you with your good works, my dear."

A happy thought struck Louisa. "Perhaps they'll play whist with the General."

"I hope they may," said Richard, laughing. "That would be an act of charity indeed."

He left the Parsonage shortly afterwards. It was a pleasantly weathered stone building, seen from the outside, not nearly as old as the church, but much older than the square, solid Dower House, intended for the widowed mothers of a succession of baronets. Sir Richard's mother was dead, and the house had been let for the last ten years to General St. John Boyce, who lived there with his wife and granddaughter. Beyond the Dower House was Bell Cottage.

No one could possibly have mistaken this tiny house for a farm labourer's dwelling. It was a perfect *cottage orné*, complete with a tiled porch and a charming circular bay. Lattice windows peeped out from under the absurdly steep roof, and there was even a miniature belfry among the convoluted chimneys.

Captain Bowyer, a naval friend of Richard's, had been rusticating here on half-pay; now he had been appointed to command a ship on the West Indies station, and the cottage had been standing empty for several weeks. Richard opened the low gate and walked up the narrow path (everything here was on a very small scale). He noted a gutter full of leaves and a broken windowpane, as well as the pale, scented primroses in their green frills that clustered round his feet. He wondered whether it did sound rather odd—an unknown lady wanting to come and rent a house in an isolated village she had never seen. Going round the cottage to the garden at the back, he discovered he was not alone.

Sitting on a wrought iron seat under a weeping

ash tree there was a tall, rather plump girl in bright pink pelisse, busily drawing in a sketchbook. She was General Boyce's granddaughter, from the Dower House, and her name was Harriet Piper.

She jumped to her feet when she saw him. "Oh, Sir Richard: good morning. I'm trespassing, I hope you don't mind—"

"You can come here as often as you like, Harriet, while the cottage is empty—so long as you don't take a chill in this uncertain weather."

"I shan't do that," she assured him, her large, brown, trustful eyes sparkling with good health and friendliness. "Is it true that Verney is coming home at last? Will he be here all the summer?"

Richard was not anxious to encourage Harriet's interest in his scapegrace brother. He said repressively that although Verney was expected before dinner, he was not likely to stay long in the country. "He never has, you know, since he joined the Army."

"He's left the Army, hasn't he? Grandpapa says—"

She stopped, and Richard noticed with some amusement that even Harriet felt a certain awkwardness about repeating Grandpapa's comments on a young man who threw up a military career when he might have been killing Frenchmen.

"Yes, Verney has sent in his papers," he said in a matter-of-fact manner that brooked no further questions. "And I must be on my way to the stables. Good morning, Harriet."

2

After Sir Richard had disappeared round the corner of Bell Cottage, Harriet was left to meditate on their short conversation, uncomfortably aware that he had thought her vulgarly curious and perhaps impertinent. All her life she had been scolded for blurting things out that she had better have left unsaid. Well, it was no good crying over this particular saucer of spilt milk. She took refuge in her sketchbook. She had always wanted to draw Bell Cottage from this particular angle. There was a beautiful thick shadow from the lintel of the dining room window, and the whole aspect could be made delightfully mysterious.

She had been taught drawing at school as an accomplishment, and contrary to most young ladylike accomplishments it had become a true pleasure, one she enjoyed even more than reading. She was never lonely when she was drawing or painting, which was just as well, for she spent a great deal of her time alone. There was no real companionship to be had from either of her grandparents.

General St. John Boyce had served in the war against the American colonies, and in various other places where both fame and glory had eluded him. He was an indolent man, he had a reasonable income, and he was content to live at Wardley as Sir Richard Capel's tenant in order to escape the tedium of being responsible for any property of his own. His wife was interested in her appearance, her comfort and her food, and by the time Harriet knew her, in very little else.

Harriet was the eldest daughter of their only child Henrietta, who as a beautiful girl of seventeen had caught the fancy of an East India merchant more than twice her age. To do them justice, the Boyces were not mercenary. They had not much liked the match, but Henrietta was determined to be rich and cut a dash; she made life so intolerable that her parents speedily gave in. Once married to her nabob she was thoroughly miserable. She disliked her

13

husband more and more, and this unfortunately affected her feelings for their little girl. When Piper died, in 1798, she dumped the child with her mother and promptly remarried, this time for love. Her second husband was a soldier; with him she was perfectly content to follow the drum, taking their growing tribe of children along with her, but there were always reasons why it was not suitable for Harriet to join them: the journey would be too difficult—their present house was too small—regimental society was no place for an unmarried girl. Just now they were in Ireland, and Mrs. Feltham had found a splendid new loophole: Harriet had to stay at Wardley and be a comfort to her grandmother.

Harriet had seen through these excuses long ago. At eight years old she had announced: "Mama doesn't love me." It was one of her earliest efforts at blurting out, and she had been punished by her governess for being wicked and ungrateful, so on this subject at least she had learnt to keep her mouth shut, but she knew very well that her mother did not love her, and that although her grandparents tolerated her presence, they did not greatly care whether she was there or not. They were never unkind, simply indifferent. She had been sent to an expensive Bath boarding school (paid for by her trustees out of the moderate fortune left her by her father). Now she had come out as a grown-up young lady, there was no more school, and the days at the Dower House sometimes seemed very long.

She went home at about one o'clock, her sketch completed and her feet numb because she had been quite oblivious of the cold spring breeze. Her grandfather was sitting in his study with the door open, reading the newspaper, a sallow man with a

14

pronounced stoop. He asked her where she had been, for the sake of saying something, not because he wanted to know.

"In the next garden, sir. I made a drawing of the cottage."

"That's a good girl," he said vaguely, rustling the pages of the *Morning Post*.

Upstairs she found her grandmother installed in the drawing room where luncheon was laid on a side table, a light, informal repast for anyone who needed some refreshment between breakfast at ten and dinner at half-past four. Mrs. Boyce was a pretty old lady with snow white hair which looked very much as it must have done in her youth, when it was fashionable to wear powder. She did not ask where Harriet had been, having preoccupations of her own.

"I wish I was not obliged to go to Mrs. Porter's card party. That house is always so draughty, and you know I cannot abide draughts."

"Perhaps she'll put you next to the fire, Grandmama." Harriet was inspecting the sandwich tray.

"Pour me another glass of wine, my love, if you will."

Harriet did as she was asked, saying: "I met Sir Richard this morning, and it's true they are expecting Verney home today."

"So your grandfather was telling me."

Mrs. Boyce put on quite a sagacious expression, as though she was on the point of making an important comment. Presently she made it.

"The flavour of this ham is not so good as the last one."

After luncheon Harriet went into her bedroom. She did not know what to do with herself; she needed a break from drawing, she had finished her library book—there was always the pianoforte, but Grandmama did not like her practising at this hour, which suited Harriet, who was not really musical and did not like practising at any hour. Fidgetting around the room, she caught sight of herself in the tipped cheval glass. An unusually tall girl, she'd inherited that from her father. Perhaps it was her height that baffled those exquisite, small women, her mother and grandmother? Junoesque, thought Harriet, that's how they describe very tall females. And very fat females too. But I'm not fat, she decided indignantly, craning at herself in the glass to make sure this was true, and observing with dislike the pink and white solidity of her neck and arms, and the way her dress was strained taut above the high waist. I'm not *fat*, precisely. If only I didn't take up so much space.

Her countenance was good and her dark eyes were rather striking. Her hair was cut short in a modish crop which was very becoming to her particular style. She wondered how she would appear to a stranger, or to someone who had not seen her for a year or more. To Verney Capel, for instance.

An idea struck her. She put on her bonnet and pelisse, ran downstairs and out of the front door. She crossed the stretch of grass at the front, which was known as Church Green, and began to walk slowly up the drive towards the Hall. On her left there fanned out a beautiful grove of trees which marked the outer edge of the celebrated Wardley pleasure gardens designed sixty years ago by Sir Richard's grandfather. There was an ornamental lake which was Harriet's favourite haunt, and which she was always trying to paint. But she was not going to the lake today; she had another object in view. She continued steadily up the drive, which presently curled round in a calculated loop so that a stranger would come quite suddenly on the first, fine prospect of Wardley Hall. It was no surprise to Harriet, yet it always gave her a fresh sense of satisfaction, the grey stone mansion built in the last century on the site of a much older house. The façade was plain and regular, with the great central portico striking a single note of drama. The sky-line at roof level was fretted by a long balustrade, surmounted by a row of urns, and rising above them again, immediately over the portico, the slender curves of a graceful cupola. The house was set in open parkland, with a ha-ha dividing it from the fields where Sir Richard grew his corn and barley, and the meadows where he pastured his cattle and sheep.

Harriet had come as far as she intended; she had no wish to be spied on from the Hall. She retraced her steps for about two hundred yards, then turned and strolled up the drive again to the place where she had stopped before. At first she kept assuring herself that this was a perfectly legitimate way of taking the air, but after she had repeated the performance three times she began to feel quite oppressed by the indelicacy of what she was doing—hanging about deliberately in order to cast herself in the way of a young man.

She was just about to give up and go home when she caught the sound she had been waiting for: the even clop of two well-matched horses approaching up the drive. A moment later Verney Capel's curricle came into view, shaped like a cockleshell, high-sprung between its two huge wheels, and drawn by a smart pair of bays.

Harriet stepped forward impulsively. The nearside horse was startled by the pink pelisse and made a violent attempt to shy.

"Good God, Harriet, what do you mean by frightening my horses?" shouted Verney, angry and not at all civil, as he struggled to straighten up the curricle and get both his pair facing the same way.

Harriet was an experienced rider; she knew how stupid she had been. She gazed imploringly at Verney. He was a slender young man, as tall as Sir Richard, much fairer and not nearly so handsome, but with a quick, restless swashbuckling air that she, at any rate, found very engaging.

"I'm sorry, Verney," she faltered. "You took me by surprise." She was anxious to give the impression that this was a chance encounter. "I didn't expect to see you just then."

"Didn't you know I was coming home today?"

"Oh yes, we all knew that," said Harriet honestly. (It was something he would probably find out from Sir Richard.)

To her consternation he looked suddenly furious.

"I might have guessed that my reputation would get here ahead of me." The words were as bitter as they were obscure. "Well, I can't keep my beasts standing in the cold."

He just tipped the brim of his beaver hat, and before she could gather her wits together he had driven on.

She gazed miserably after him. In their imaginary meeting she had seen herself astonishing him with her newfound elegance and ease of manner. Instead she had been clumsy and inept. Once again she had offended someone she admired, and to make it worse, she hadn't the faintest idea why.

3

When Verney reached the Hall, he went straight up to the room he had occupied since he was a boy, and stayed there talking to Stokes, his brother's valet, who had come to unpack for him, until it was time to change for dinner. They had always dined at five: Stokes informed him that the young ladies (his nieces Kitty and Chloe) were now promoted to dine with their father—and Master Dick too, of course; he was home from Eton for the holidays. Verney decided that he would prefer to get his first meeting with Richard over before they were launched on an evening of schoolroom insipidity. So he dressed early and left his bedchamber at precisely half-past four.

The house was so quiet he might have been the only person alive. He trod sedately down the grand staircase, a superb flight of shallow stone steps, flooded with light from the glazed cupola overhead. Dominating the staircase wall was a Van Dyck portrait of the first Sir Richard Capel cavorting on his horse in front of the dark, cramped manor house which his descendants had very sensibly pulled down. Verney crossed the hall (which was paved with squares of black and white marble, like a chessboard) turned along a short corridor and made his way to the red anteroom.

It was here that the family always assembled before dinner. As he expected, he was the first to arrive. He waited, in front of the empty fireplace, a prey to the most humiliating qualms of apprehension. He had seen Richard only once since the beginning of the trouble that had led him to resign his commission. George Sutcliffe had challenged him to a duel—a senior officer had put a stop to that—but still some well-meaning busybody had notified Richard, who had come dashing up to London to find out what was going on. Verney, feeling he could not bear the reproaches of his virtuous elder brother had deliberately avoided him. He had left Richard's letters unanswered and behaved in an altogether childish manner. The day they finally met, he happened to be rather drunk, which had seemed providential at the time.

But he had merely put off the evil hour, and this evening he was painfully sober.

He heard the familiar footsteps in the corridor, pulled himself up a little straighter. And here was Richard, entirely self-possessed as always, urbanely hoping he'd had a good journey.

"Very pleasant, thank you, sir." Verney was resentfully aware that he sounded fulsome and nervous.

"I am sorry I was out when you arrived; I had to ride over to Spargrove." There was a slight pause. Apparently Richard had nothing more to say.

He too had changed into evening dress, black coat and pantaloons, with a white waistcoat which was particularly suited to his air of quiet self-command and impeccable breeding. There was a gap of fourteen years between the brothers: when their father died Richard had been nineteen and Verney five, so in a sense Richard had played the part of a father, the ideal arbiter whose praise or censure was the only judgment Verney cared about in the long run.

"I hope you didn't mind me coming," he began, disconcerted by his noncommittal reception. "You

20

know what I'm supposed to have done. I wanted the chance to explain—"

"I know what you admitted to your Colonel," said Richard bleakly. "There's nothing further to be said. The sooner the whole wretched business is forgotten the better."

Ten minutes ago Verney would have been grateful to be let down so lightly; now he experienced a curious disappointment. He felt that he needed Richard to treat him quite differently—and Richard ought to have known.

"I don't see how it can be forgotten," he said rather sulkily, "if I'm to be an object of curiosity to the entire village."

"Why should you be? It seems most unlikely."

"Don't they all know why I was forced to leave the regiment?"

"Certainly not. Theo and Louisa know, of course, but you cannot suppose we should have let the news spread among the servants or the tenants, and who else is there? Bell Cottage is empty at present and the Boyces are wrapped up in their own concerns—"

"Then why was Harriet Piper waiting in the drive, all agog to stare at me as I came by?"

"Was she?" Richard was plainly annoyed. "Well, she is a silly girl—"

"And she said in a very pointed way that they all knew I was expected."

"My dear Verney, surely you can imagine what Harriet was after—however, that's neither here nor there." Richard apparently thought better of what he was going to say. "No doubt some of our more worldly neighbours may get hold of a few scraps of London gossip sooner or later, but the talk will soon die down."

Verney was not listening; he had just caught the

drift of Richard's previous remark. He remembered how Harriet had pursued him with a far from secret admiration when she was a little girl; he might have recognised the symptoms today, if he hadn't been so preoccupied. It was absurd to find that the amazon in the pink pelisse was still so unguarded— and so faithful. He could not help being touched.

"I've had a famous idea," he remarked with an assumed jauntiness. "I shall stay here and marry the she-nabob."

"I knew the army hadn't improved you, Verney," said Richard in a voice of cold dislike. "I didn't know your conversation had become so regrettably second-rate. Marry the she-nabob, indeed! What a charming prospect for the poor girl. I am amazed by your condescension."

"Good God, I wasn't serious."

"I'm glad to hear it. The less you see of Harriet Piper the better."

"Why, what's wrong with her?"

"Nothing. There is enough wrong with you, however, to make you a most unsuitable friend and companion for a young, inexperienced and impulsive girl whose family don't take as much care of her as they should. She has a forward manner, which is chiefly due to ignorance, but it renders her particularly vulnerable. I don't believe you would want to marry her for her money; I'm quite sure you don't want to marry her without it. And if no marriage is in question, to put it plainly, you would be wise to keep out of her way."

"You must be mad!" Verney was now very red in the face. "Are you suggesting that I would deliberately seduce one of our nearest neighbours whom I've known ever since she was a child?"

"You knew Pamela Rokeby when she was in her

cradle," retorted Richard. "You met George Sutcliffe on your first day at Eton. Neither of these facts seem to have weighed on your conscience three months ago."

Verney opened his mouth and shut it again. What was the use of arguing? He now knew that Richard, like everyone else, saw him as an unprincipled rake, a corrupter of innocence. And in spite of all appearances, this was completely unjustified. It was true that George and Pamela Sutcliffe had been married less than a year and that Pamela was only nineteen, so ethereal, so modest and (unlike Harriet) so well brought-up—it had taken Verney some time to recognise how cleverly she had used these qualities as a weapon to tease and incite him, and the artless simplicity with which she had faltered out those shocking stories about poor old George. Once she had become his mistress, Verney soon lost his illusions about her, but he was totally unprepared for what happened next. Without warning, and with no reason that he could see, Pamela had made a dramatic confession. In a hubbub of hysteria, remorse and spurious martyrdom, she had thrown herself on her husband's mercy—and Verney to the wolves. He had made no attempt to defend himself, he knew the rules: having behaved like a scoundrel, he was expected to bear the consequences like a gentleman. He was, after all, in the wrong. But the whole episode had profoundly disturbed his faith in women. What demon of wicked mischief or sick fantasy could have driven Pamela to act in such a way? She had lied about him, she had lied about George, she had carried on like a creature possessed. He had not felt able to tell the truth about her, or to discuss her frankly, with anyone in London. He had hoped

23

that it would be possible to talk to Richard, and that however angry Richard was, he might be prepared to listen, and perhaps to resolve the enigma of Pamela.

Well that had been a piece of stupidity. There was no comfort or understanding to be had from Richard, who had rigid ideas about the sanctity of marriage, and who was bound to think him the greatest villain unhung if he laid the blame on poor little Pamela, so much more sinned against than sinning. Richard had always put women on a pedestal. He had married early and happily, he had loved and cherished Catherine until the day she died (even though she had spent her last years as a very exacting invalid) and he was still an unconsoled widower. His own experience, grafted on to a natural idealism, had made him altogether too highminded to condone the failings of ordinary mortals. He's done his duty, thought Verney bitterly. He's warned me not to ruin Harriet. I wonder I'm allowed to sit at table with his own daughters.

They had just appeared in the doorway, two pretty, fair-haired girls in white muslin dresses, shepherded by their governess, Miss Pringle.

"Dear Uncle Verney, we haven't seen you for an age," said fifteen-year-old Kitty. She was the eldest of Richard's four children, the one who most resembled their mother and felt her loss most keenly. "It is very comfortable to have you home again," she added, in her grave little voice. "Isn't it, Papa?"

"Yes, indeed," said Richard, not looking at his brother.

Verney greeted his other niece, Chloe, a lively fourteen-year-old who was a complete contrast to good, serious Kitty. Her bubbling enthusiasm was drowned in the noisy and breathless arrival of Master Dick Capel, who knew he was late for dinner.

Dick was thirteen, and his gift for growing like a beanstalk surprised Verney every time they met. Apparently it also surprised Richard, Louisa or whoever had the ordering of his clothes, for nothing he wore ever seemed long enough.

He surveyed his favourite uncle with unabashed curiosity. "Are you pleased to be out of the Army? I can see the Guards must be pretty tame, with all those parades and reviews, but why didn't you exchange into a Hussar regiment? That's what I'd have done."

"Dick, don't be impertinent," said his father.

"I'm sorry, sir," said Dick cheerfully. He was on his usual Tom Tiddler's ground, seeing how far he could go.

Richard had always managed the boy very skilfully; Verney wondered whether he would be so successful when Dick was nineteen or twenty. He was himself conscious of having grown away from Richard in the last two or three years. There was this deep chasm of reserve between them now, in areas of conduct that had been irrelevant during his childhood.

4

Harriet had a standing invitation to visit Kitty and Chloe whenever she chose. She was often quite glad to do so, even though she was a grown-up young lady and the Capel girls were still in the schoolroom, and on the morning after Verney's arrival she felt irresistibly drawn towards the Hall. She set off about eleven o'clock; it was a fine April morning, and she was conscious of looking her best in a new yellow walking dress and a spencer jacket.

When she arrived at the gravel sweep in front of the great portico, she met the sisters and Miss Pringle just coming out. They were going to walk round the lake, and asked Harriet to join them. She accepted, casting a regretful glance at the house; it would have suited her better if they had stayed indoors.

However, there was nothing she could do but fall into step beside Kitty as they crossed the wide stretch of lawn which extended along the western wing of the Hall. This was a short cut to the pleasure gardens.

"How is Ned?" asked Harriet. "I hope his cough is better?"

"Yes, he is almost recovered. Mr. Flyte is very pleased with him."

Ned was eight years old, the youngest of the family, and a constant anxiety. It was soon after his birth that Lady Capel's health had begun to fail, and perhaps Ned had inherited a constitutional weakness, for although he was a bright, intelligent little boy he had always been delicate.

Kitty and Miss Pringle told Harriet about a new treatment which the apothecary had recommended.

"I wish he would recommend something sensible like sea-bathing," remarked Chloe. "Then perhaps Papa would take a house at Brighton and we should see Prinny and all the dandies."

"I cannot imagine your Papa doing anything of the sort," said Miss Pringle crushingly. "And pray do not let me hear you speak of His Royal Highness in that disrespectful manner."

They had now got to a place where the lawn began to roll away under their feet in a steep decline. They stood still, looking down into another world.

It was a world of extraordinary beauty. In the year 1750 Sir Edward Capel had been inspired to transform this bleak upland valley into the kind of landscape he had learnt to admire on the Grand Tour. It was a generous act of faith, for he could never have lived long enough to see his slow-growing masterpiece in its romantic perfection as his descendants were seeing it now, with the folds of mature woodland sweeping down to the crystal waters of a solitary lake. The trees had been grouped with infinite care, each one chosen in relation to its neighbours, so that the differences in outline and colour, and in the very shape and texture of the leaves, provided a fascinating contrast. This variety was already visible in the spring, and would become richer and more vivid as the summer drew on to autumn. The lake was shaped like an hourglass, and spanned at its narrowest point by a so-called Rustic Bridge, a carved stone affair, which had a wrought iron trellis overhead, festooned with ivy and other climbing plants. The bridge was immediately below the place where they were standing and quite close to it there was a pretty stone pavilion decorated with a riot of tiny pointed turrets that looked just like candle snuffers. This was Lady Adela's Bower, named after an heiress who was supposed to have lived at Wardley in the Middle Ages. Over on the other side of the lake there was a rather gloomy looking folly known as the Nunnery. Sir Edward had built the Rustic Bridge and the Nunnery, his son had contributed Lady Adela's Bower.

Harriet and the schoolroom party were halfway down the path that led into the valley when a voice hailed them from above. They turned and saw

27

a man in a blue coat at the top of the grassy slope.

It was Verney.

"Good morning!" He called out as he came closer. "I saw you from the library window, and I knew at once that a walk round the lake was the very thing I needed. May I come with you?"

He made his request to Miss Pringle but one brief glance at Harriet somehow gave her the idea that she was the person who had lured him out of the library.

Suddenly elated, she said, "I hope your horse has got over the fright I gave him yesterday."

"He was shockingly ungallant, wasn't he? And so was I. But you must remember we are two poor, stupid cockneys who don't know how to go on in the country."

His lively hazel eyes were full of laughter, but it was kind laughter, the teasing of affection. He went on looking at her, and she felt her heart thumping deliciously.

"What do you mean?" demanded Chloe, who was listening all ears. "When did Harriet frighten your horse, and why are you ungallant?"

Her uncle took no notice of this question, very much to Harriet's relief. Instead he asked about the young black and white dog that was frisking around their feet, galloping on ahead and then dashing back again.

"I don't recognise this fellow: what do you call him?"

"Sam. He's one of dear old Sally's pups."

They had reached the water's edge, and bore right-handed, away from the Rustic Bridge, along the path that encircled the upper section of the lake. There were birds singing in the branches overhead, swans nesting in the rushes, fish plopping in the sun-dappled pools; the world was awake and teeming with new life.

Chloe picked up a short stick and threw it for Sam; she said she was teaching him to retrieve. Sam was perfectly willing to run after sticks, though he didn't always bring them back. He hid them in the bushes, or dropped them to bark at one of the swans that was sliding past on the surface of the water. The swan ignored him, silent and supercilious.

Presently they reached the top of the lake, where the stream that brought in a constant supply of fresh water had been cleverly directed through a miniature mountain landscape of highly dramatic rocks and boulders. The bottom of the lake had been scooped out so that the stream was finally able to splash downwards in quite a respectable waterfall, which was known as the Cascade. They stopped to admire the torrent of perpetual movement, hissing and sparkling against the blackness of the rocks.

In front of them, a little closer than the Cascade, was Sir Edward Capel's greatest achievement, his underwater Grotto. It was not literally under the water, being excavated out of the bank at a level a little lower than the surface of the lake.

"Let's go inside," said Harriet, leading the way down a short flight of steps which plunged into a chamber about twelve feet square. The single window was a jagged fissure high up in the rock face which formed the outer wall of the Grotto, and the light that crept in was reflected off the bubbling water only a few inches below, so that it shimmered and wavered in elusive rings over the inside of the cavern, which was thickly encrusted with shells. There were thousands of shells: bone white, sullen pewter or creamy pink, each one as perfect as a cameo. Fragments of quartz glittered between them, and flowering stems of coral. It was like being in a palace on the ocean bed, and the uneven quality of the light increased the illusion of underwater strangeness and enchantment.

"I suppose the Siren is still asleep in her bath," remarked Verney.

They all trooped into the inner chamber, which was very dim. It was just possible to see the shallow, lead-lined basin containing the recumbent statue which Sir Edward had brought home from Italy, and which his descendants knew as the Sleeping Siren. Her marble features were deathly still and her limbs were stained with green; when she was a child Harriet had been frightened of the drowned lady who lay under the water with her eyes tight shut.

Miss Pringle gave a little cough. "Come, girls. We must not dawdle here too long."

It struck Harriet that she might consider it improper for them to be looking at the statue of a naked female while in the company of a gentleman. A low laugh from Verney suggested that he had drawn the same conclusion, and they exchanged a glance of conspiratorial amusement.

Having now reached the western end of the lake, they began their return journey along the opposite bank. They soon came to the Nunnery with its narrow, pointed windows mottled in coloured glass.

"Do you remember," Harriet said to Verney, "how you and Tom Daly once tried to build a sort of prison in there and put me inside it? I must have been eight years old and I suppose you were thirteen."

"Yes, we'd been reading some horrid romance or other, and wanted to see if it was possible to wall

30

up a nun. Which I am persuaded is a great deal more difficult than people think; you were a most disobliging victim—you would do nothing but wriggle and complain that there were spiders."

"Poor Harriet!" protested Kitty. "How could you be so cruel, Uncle Verney? A little girl of eight?"

"Harriet didn't mind," he said cheerfully.

Harriet did not contradict him. She could still recall the darkness and the fusty smell in the roughcast cells where they had tried to box her in. She had felt sick with apprehension—and yet it was true that she hadn't minded. She had been too awestruck at being allowed to play with two great school boys, even on those terms, and she was practically certain all along that Verney wouldn't go away and leave her to the spiders.

"It must have been a very interesting game," said Chloe, with a touch of envy.

She picked up another stick and threw it for Sam. It fell in the water, but the dog went gamely in after it. He got it in his teeth and started to swim back towards the shore. Watching his proud little head bobbing up and down, Harriet thought how strange it was that dogs could swim by instinct and were perfectly acclimatised to water. At the very same moment she realised that Sam was no longer moving. He had struck a patch of weed just where he was trying to come ashore. He was only a foot or so from the bank, but his hind legs appeared to be caught. He dropped the stick and gave a pitiful whimper, his eyes rolling in panic. Harriet did not stop to think; she ran impetuously down the bank. Kneeling on the wet grass, she reached out to catch Sam by his front paws. He struggled to raise himself, licking her fingers, but the reeds had him fast.

31

For a perilous instant she thought she was going to join him in the lake.

Then two strong hands gripped her by the shoulders, and she heard Verney behind her saying: "Hold on—I won't let you fall."

There was a sucking noise and between them they managed to lift the little dog out of the water. Harriet found herself clasping his dripping body against her new spencer. Sam kicked ungratefully and jumped out of her arms.

"That was a very foolish thing to do," said Verney. "Once you lost your balance you might have drowned."

"Oh, I feel sure you would have rescued me," said Harriet airily.

She had discovered that being dragged up a bank by Verney was even better than being a walled-up nun. Kitty was calling her a heroine, while Chloe was tearfully fondling her pet and blaming herself for the accident. Miss Pringle struck a note of practical good sense.

"I am sure you should go home immediately, Miss Piper, and change your dress. You do not want to catch cold."

"You are perfectly right, Miss Pringle," said Verney. "Don't delay, Harriet. I'll take you back to the Dower House."

It was on the tip of Harriet's tongue to say that she didn't need an escort when she realised that she would be throwing away the chance of a most agreeable tête-à-tête.

They set off together at a brisk pace, Harriet squelching at every step, for her boots were full of water. Her new dress was streaked with mud, but she did not care. She was only sorry Verney insisted on walking so fast, which made it impossible to have a proper conversation.

They were crossing the drive when Mrs. Theo Capel came out of the Parsonage with a basket on her arm.

She had not seen her brother-in-law since his arrival, and the sight of him now, with Harriet in her stained skirt and wet boots, was the cause of so many conflicting sensations that she hardly knew what to say first.

Verney greeted her cordially and explained that Harriet had rescued Chloe's puppy from the lake and got herself pretty well soaked in the process.

"That was very well done of you, Harriet. I hope your new dress may not be entirely spoilt." Louisa frequently advised Harriet about her clothes and knew every item in her wardrobe. "You had better go straight in and change. Verney, you can give me your arm as far as the village; I am on my way to visit some of the old cottagers."

"I'm sorry, Louisa. It sounds a delightful expedition, but I'm engaged to call on General and Mrs. Boyce."

Louisa looked put out. "Surely there can be no necessity—"

"You would not wish me to be lacking in civility to Harriet's grandparents?"

And with this, he made good his escape.

Harriet was pleased and flattered. As she did not know the circumstances which had brought him back to Wardley, she had no idea that Verney was trying to avoid being preached at by his sister-in-law, and was even prepared to run the risk of hearing General Boyce's favourite dissertation on the Battle of Bunker Hill.

He was in luck, however. The General had gone

33

out and Mrs. Boyce was not yet down. Harriet left him alone in the drawing room and fled to change her wet clothes, promising to be back in five minutes.

Having nothing better to do, Verney contemplated the events of the morning. Harriet had been right in thinking that he had come after her deliberately. He had done so to annoy Richard. He had not forgiven Richard for last night's insult, and when they both saw Harriet from the library window he could not resist a wicked determination to go chasing after her, right under the nose of his high-minded brother. He had no serious intentions of any sort, certainly no desire to hurt this large, bold, impulsive girl who had about as much idea how to look after herself as that young dog of Chloe's. Thinking of the dog, however, made him consider Harriet in a rather different light. He had admired her quickness and courage in going to Sam's rescue. And afterwards, with her bonnet over one eye and mud on her skirt, she had not dissolved into a flutter, as many girls would have done, exclaiming that she must look a perfect fright, and wanting to be contradicted. She had even stopped trying too anxiously to please him, and in an unusual way he had thought her almost handsome. Brave, healthy, honest and transparent—he could not imagine a creature more unlike Pamela Sutcliffe.

There was a folio lying on the pianoforte. He opened it idly and found that it was full of Harriet's sketches. As he ruffled through them, he was surprised to discover a degree of sensibility that he would not have expected. Her drawings of the pleasure gardens were elegant and exact, as the drawings of young ladies were supposed to be, but there was a rarer quality, an evocation of melan-

34

choly and mystery in her attenuated Gothic buildings, her dense shadows, her tall trees reflected in deep water. If the boisterous Harriet could produce work like this, she must have a more interesting mind that he had ever supposed.

"I did not know you were such an accomplished artist," he said, when she came back into the room.

Harriet did not simper. She said, "I wish I could paint properly. There's a landscape in the dining room at the Hall which shows you how a real artist might execute such scenes."

"You mean the Claude? They say my grandfather designed his garden with that picture in mind. You have a discerning eye."

Harriet glowed with pleasure, but he no longer took this either as a tribute to his vanity or as a warning. He decided that she had grown into a very good sort of girl, and that it was agreeable to meet someone who wasn't going to disapprove of him.

5

Harriet was in love. This was nothing new, of course: she had been in love with Verney, in one sense or another, for the last ten years. During the long intervals when he was not available for hero-worship she had formed equally hopeless attachments for the brothers of several of her school friends. Once she had come out and started going to balls, she had expected that some romantic adventures would come her way, but her partners at the Southbury Assemblies had proved an insipid set.

Now, at last, she could claim that she loved, with

all the serious implications of the grown-up world, a young man who gave every sign of returning her affection, and who must be considered a suitable person for her to marry. Perhaps her father's money would have enabled her to look higher than a younger son, but her family had never exerted themselves to find a brilliant match for her, and Harriet was only a little anxious in case Verney might hang back out of diffidence. He had not made her anything like a declaration. But he was very particular in his attentions. Walking in the gardens, riding in the park, dining occasionally at the houses of their neighbours, she and Verney seemed to be engaged in a continuous private conversation which conveyed more than the words actually overheard by outsiders. This enthralling game had a fatal effect on her judgment, and she saw it as a final proof that he loved her.

Altogether it was a delightful April, and she was hardly at all dashed by the news that Bell Cottage had been let to two old maids.

This was naturally a disappointment, because Bell Cottage was the only place within walking distance, apart from the Parsonage and the Hall, where she might reasonably expect to find any congenial society. Most of her friends lived in the manor houses or rectories of other villages scattered around the market town of Southbury. Bell Cottage, so conveniently near, was unluckily too small for the kind of family that would have suited Harriet. The Bowyers, a childless married couple, were now to be succeeded by an elderly lady and her companion. It was not an exciting prospect.

All the same, Harriet was sufficiently interested, on the morning of their arrival, to remain with her nose pressed to her bedroom window for half an hour, watching a wagonload of furniture being carried into the cottage.

The two wagoners were assisted by the gardener and maids who had formerly worked for the Bowyers, and who were staying on with the new tenants. Up and down the little path they went, carrying tables and chairs, dismantled beds and corded boxes, and also such items as a bath full of pots and pans, and a clock wrapped up in a blanket. The furniture was not new but it looked good. Harriet was surprised to see a harp.

Presently a post chaise and four came spanking through the drive gates and pulled up behind the wagon. Like all such conveyances, it was a travelling chariot that had once belonged to a private family but was now painted yellow to show that it was let out for hire. One of the postilions got off his horse and went round to open the door. Out stepped a weather-beaten lady of about fifty, presumably Miss Johnson.

Another person jumped lightly down behind her —quite a young lady this time, slender and graceful. This must be the paid companion, poor creature. Though she did not look in the slightest degree pathetic, wearing that absurd and charming hat with a bunch of cherries under the brim. Her clear voice floated up to Harriet, full of warmth and pleasure.

"Did you ever see such a cottage, ma'am? We shall feel like a pair of spellbound princesses in a fairy tale."

They went indoors. A belch of thick, damp smoke came out of one of the chimneys. Apparently the kitchen fire was giving trouble, for Harriet heard the cook shouting something to the gardener about birds' nests. How uncomfortable it must be, moving house. She knew it would be vulgarly curious and ill-bred to call on perfect strangers before they were ready to receive visitors, but surely one might make a neighbourly offer of assistance? It was no use asking her grandmother, so she thought she would consult Mrs. Theo Capel, who always did what was right with enviable self-assurance.

She might have felt less friendly towards the Rector's wife if she could have overheard a conversation that was taking place in the breakfast parlour at the Parsonage.

"I wish Verney would be a little more circumspect," Louisa was saying to Richard. "He ought to mind what he is about, paying such marked attentions to Harriet. Not that I believe there is anything in the slightest degree wrong—but she is an ignorant, empty-headed girl who gets all her ideas of life from reading novels, and I am afraid she will soon convince herself that he is in love with her."

Richard did not answer at once. He had dropped in to see Theo, who was out, and had remained, as he often did, for a chat with Louisa. But his thoughts seemed rather disjointed this morning, as he stood with his hands in his pockets gazing out of the window.

"Could you not give him a hint?" suggested his sister-in-law.

"I'm afraid my hints are the very reason for his wanting to flirt with her."

"What do you mean?"

Richard told her of that acrimonious exchange on the night of Verney's return, and how he had warned his brother to keep away from Harriet—unwisely, as it turned out. "For whatever scrapes he may have got into in London, he has never behaved improperly with the young, unmarried daughters of our friends and neighbours here. I hurt his pride and he is paying me out."

"There is no need for him to pay Harriet out at the same time. Unless he seriously wishes to marry her. That would be coals of fire on your head, wouldn't it?"

"Verney marry Harriet? Good God, I hope not! It would be disastrous."

"Why do you object?" asked Louisa. She was surprised. There was nothing the matter with Harriet that could not be cured by time and good advice. And she had an independent fortune.

"He does not love her," said Richard, by way of explanation.

"Not everyone can marry for love."

"Very true. There are marriages of mild affection that turn out extremely well, but as a rule the sentiments are about equal on each side. Harriet is far too plainly in love, besides being so young; how would she get on with a man who simply married her for her money? She would be wretched, and his faults would grow worse as a consequence. No, it would not answer."

"I dare say you are right." There was a slight pause before she asked, "What are you looking at, out of the window?"

"At nothing in particular. There is a post chaise in front of Bell Cottage, but my new tenants are not on view."

"Oh, have they arrived? The wagon was here by seven, and I am told the two ladies were spending last night in Southbury. So as to be early on the premises this morning, I suppose."

"It must be a fatiguing business," said Richard, unconsciously echoing Harriet. "I wonder, should I go across and make myself known to them? In case they need any assistance?"

"What sort of assistance should they want? I dare say they would far rather be left in peace."

"Well, I don't know. Two ladies on their own, and no longer young, for they are friends of Bowyer's mother, you know—"

"All the more reason to treat them with formality. They are bound to be at sixes and sevens, with their hair standing on end and not a chair in the place ready to sit down on. I am sure they are not in the mood for meeting anyone, least of all Sir Richard Capel!"

"My dear Louisa, I'm not the Prince Regent!" he protested.

She could see that he was determined to make himself useful. He was exceptionally considerate towards others, besides being far too unaffected to imagine that his own great wealth and position might sometimes make him an embarrassing visitor.

Louisa was quite anxious to meet the new tenants, though she thought it beneath her dignity to say so. She accompanied Richard out of the Parsonage, and they were approaching Bell Cottage when Harriet ran down the steps of the Dower House to join them. She wanted to know whether she should call on Miss Johnson with an offer of hot water or anything else that was required.

"They might be glad of the water if the fires aren't drawing properly, only I don't want to put myself forward, and I thought you would tell me what I ought to do."

Richard and Louisa both began to laugh.

Harriet blushed scarlet. "Have I said something stupid?"

"We weren't laughing at you," Richard assured

her quickly. "The fact is, Mrs. Capel and I have spent the last ten minutes arguing the same point. We wish to be of service but we don't like to put ourselves forward."

As he spoke, the front door of Bell Cottage opened and the weather-beaten lady came out. She could hardly avoid hearing his last few words, and there was a gleam of appreciation in her bright blue eyes as she surveyed the deputation.

Richard stepped forward immediately. If he felt a fool, he had too much poise to show it.

"Miss Johnson, I believe? May I introduce myself? I am your landlord—"

"You are mistaken, sir." The lady glanced back at someone in the shadow of the porch. "Julia, my love . . ."

Her friend moved forward into the sunlight. She had taken off her bonnet. Her hair was dark and feathery fine: her face was oval, with delicate features and brilliant grey eyes under sweeping black lashes. Her sleeves were rolled up to the elbow, she was wearing a coarse linen apron and carrying a coffeepot still wrapped in silver paper.

"I am Julia Johnson," she said in her pretty, clear voice. "And you must be Sir Richard Capel. How do you do?"

She dipped a swift curtsey, completely undismayed by her apron and the coffeepot. It was Richard who seemed at a loss; he bowed gravely, without speaking, as though he had been stunned by the sudden surprise of her beauty.

Miss Johnson said she would like to make him acquainted with Mrs. Williams, who was going to share her new home.

Richard recovered his tongue. "I hope you will both be very comfortable here. May I introduce you

41

to my sister-in-law, Mrs. Capel? You will soon be meeting my brother, who is the Rector of the parish. And this is Miss Harriet Piper, the nearest of your neighbours, for she lives just over that hedge."

"Surely you can't have been a friend of Captain Bowyer's mother," said Harriet, with her well-known propensity for speaking out of turn.

Julia Johnson seemed rather taken aback, but her reply was perfectly good-humoured. "Is that what you were told? How very ridiculous. His mother was at school with *my* mother. That is the connection."

"Oh, I see," mumbled Harriet, aware that she had been impertinent, and that both Sir Richard and Mrs. Capel were disapproving of her. She had been astonished to find that Miss Johnson was a beautiful woman somewhere between twenty-five and thirty years old. What was her history? Why wasn't she married? What could have induced her to come and bury herself in this obscure corner of Wiltshire? These questions were certainly not going to be answered here and now. But the arrival of such a neighbour promised to make this spring at Wardley even more interesting than it was already.

6

As soon as the incoming tenants were settled at Bell Cottage, Mrs. Boyce paid them a formal call, taking Harriet with her. Harriet was charmed with their new acquaintance, who turned out to be everything she had hoped for.

"Miss Johnson is so very agreeable," she confided in Verney. "I never met anyone who could make friends so easily. Not that she is over-eager—she

42

has a good deal of reserve about her own affairs, I fancy, and I'm sure she would never be intrusive, her manners are far too good—but there is a way of being interested without being curious, you know, and Miss Johnson seems to have the knack. I believe she kept house for her father; he was a clergyman and he died two or three years ago. I wonder how old she is."

"I am surprised you didn't ask her."

"I am not so gauche as I used to be." In fact, Harriet was trying to emulate the well-mannered Miss Johnson, and she had managed to collect quite a lot of information without asking questions. "Mrs. Williams is the widow of a naval officer. I think they must be old family friends. The furniture belongs to Miss Johnson, and she has brought such a stack of books with her: history and philosophy, as well as poetry. And she can play the harp."

"A very suitable occupation for the daughter of a clergyman."

"How absurd you are," said Harriet happily.

They were out driving in Verney's curricle.

It was splendid to sit up there beside her handsome escort, the observed of all observers, as they bowled through Wardley village. The body of the curricle was dark blue; the wheels picked out in scarlet and the silver-mounted harness matched the colours of the Capel crest, which was painted on the side panel in silver and red. Verney's groom, perched precariously behind them, wore dark blue livery with silver buttons.

Verney drove well, with a good deal of panache. His horses were a fine match and his carriage was beautifully sprung. When he took a corner rather too sharp Harriet merely braced her feet against the dashboard (which was curved like the prow of an

43

ancient galley) and said nothing. She saw that this nonchalance met with his approval.

They passed a stretch of common land that had recently been surrounded by a stout fence. There were some men inside, clearing the ground, rooting out the tangle of bushes and briars and dead bracken. Among the labourers in their blue smock-frocks they caught sight of Sir Richard and his bailiff.

Sir Richard turned to watch the curricle go by. Verney raised his hat with a flourish and Harriet bowed graciously. After a few minutes' thought, she said: "Some people say it's wrong to enclose common land, but I don't understand why. None of the country people around here are starving."

"It depends what you do with your enclosures when you've got them."

"How do you mean?"

"There are men who simply want to enlarge their parks or preserve more pheasants, so some commoners lose their grazing rights and get nothing in exchange. But good landlords like Richard only enclose what they intend to improve. They know that clean ground provides better grazing for better stock. They bring in new breeds of cattle, and make work for more herdsmen and dairymaids. And new breeds of sheep, so there's more wool for the cottagers to spin and weave. They take on more ploughboys and sow more acres of wheat. And everyone lives a little better as a consequence. Did you never hear of Coke or Norfolk?"

"He is a famous farmer, isn't he?" she ventured, a little overwhelmed by this outburst of oratory.

"When he started his experiments there were two hundred and seventy people in the parish of Holkham; now there are over a thousand, all so prosperous that they're pulling down the workhouse because they don't need one. Richard says that if more landlords followed Coke's methods of husbandry, there would be fewer hardships blamed on the enclosures and the war."

He had reined in his horses and they were driving more slowly, so that he could point out examples of his brother's provident farming: well-hung gates, ditches that were properly dug, and long-neglected wasteland neatly planted with turnips. They made a leisurely tour, and were on their way home, not more than a mile from the Wardley gates, when Harriet said:

"I'm glad no one has improved Cory Wood. The finest cowslips in the county grow on the other side of those trees; I suppose they must be at their best this week."

He drew up beside a low stile. "Do you want to pick some?"

"Would you mind?"

"I am at your service, ma'am." Verney jumped down into the road. "Walk the horses for me, Tom. We shan't be long."

"Very good, sir."

Verney helped Harriet out of the curricle and across the stile, two manoeuvres she could have managed on her own, if she hadn't been hampered by a wretchedly fashionable skirt, and by the convention that ladies must not show their legs. Cory Wood was quite narrow at that point, and a few minutes' walk brought them into the open. A shoulder of grassland, sloping southwards, was faintly streaked with yellow, shimmering in the sun. Cowslips never made a vivid effect like primroses or bluebells; it was hard to imagine that these flesh-coloured stalks with their tiny, pale-tipped flowers

45

could be bunched together into such a glorious, butter-golden mass. Harriet began to pick, quickly and greedily, hunting for thicker stems and taller flowers while Verney strolled along beside her, picking in a more desultory manner. It was hot work. She soon unbuttoned her pelisse, and then took off her straw bonnet and turned it into a basket to carry her cowslips in.

"Haven't you got nearly enough?" asked Verney. "You look like that female in Shakespeare—"

"Perdita?" she enquired hopefully.

"Ophelia."

"Oh, that is a great deal too bad," she exclaimed, not averse to being teased, but trying surreptitiously to make herself look a little more respectable. It occurred to her suddenly that he ought not to be here at all. It was permissible to go for a drive with a young man in an open carriage, especially if you had a groom in attendance. To be alone together in a flower-strewn meadow without a soul in sight—this was quite improper. She shook back her untidy fringe, smoothed the collar of her dress. As she did so, she gave a cry of dismay.

"My locket! I've lost my locket."

It was a flat, gold pendant with the initial H in seed pearls, worn on a thin chain. Her mother had sent it to her and it contained a ring of plaited hair belonging to one of her little half-brothers.

"I must have pulled it off when I undid my coat."

"Are you sure you were wearing it?"

"I always wear it."

"But this morning perhaps you forgot—"

"No, I tell you, I always wear it. Besides, I remember wondering whether the catch was loose. What a fool I was to put it on!"

"We'd better start looking for it," he said amenably.

Which was easier said than done. They had wandered a considerable way on their flower-picking expedition, and as Harriet had been bent double most of the time, with her gaze fixed on the grass it was impossible to trace her erratic course. They had spent about a quarter of an hour collecting the cowslips, but to drag over the ground again, inch by inch, was such an endless performance that they soon lost all sense of time. Harriet began to feel frantic. The locket was particularly precious because she had so few presents from her mother. She needed the reassurance of wearing it every day, and if anyone happened to admire it, she enjoyed opening the case with her thumbnail and speaking casually of "my Mama" and "my brother," just like other girls. She was afraid her treasure had gone for good, and hardly noticed that Verney was getting restive.

"Is the locket very valuable?"

"My mama gave it to me."

From the note in her voice you might have thought her mother was dead, which irritated Verney, who knew she was in Ireland.

"Surely she won't be angry with you for losing it," he suggested. "After all, she won't know. You hardly ever see her."

Harriet's eyes filled with tears, and she gave him a glance of such tragic reproach that he immediately remembered how disgracefully Henrietta Feltham had neglected her eldest daughter. He cursed himself for being a clumsy lout.

"Don't cry, Harri." It was the name he had called her as a child. He took her arm and gave her what was intended to be a comforting, brotherly kiss on the cheek.

He felt her whole body fluctuate. She turned her head, the tears had vanished: he found himself kiss-

47

ing her soft and yielding mouth. This delightful sensation lasted the few seconds it took him to gather his wits. Then he disengaged himself with more haste than chivalry.

"I'm sorry. We—I should not have done that."

"Was it so very bad?"

"I had no business to bring you here." He glanced around for a means of escape from this dangerous privacy. They were quite close to the road again, about a quarter of a mile beyond the wood and the place where they had left the curricle.

As they stood there, they caught the clop of trotting ponies coming from the direction of Wardley, and a moment later Louisa's low phaeton came into view, with Louisa driving and Richard seated behind her wearing an extremely grim expression— which might have been partly due to the fact that he hated being driven by a woman.

The two couples eyed each other over the hedge. The phaeton halted abruptly.

"What the devil are you doing there?" demanded Richard.

"We've been picking cowslips. And hunting for a locket of Harriet's that she lost somewhere in the field."

"We were afraid you had met with an accident. It must be more than two hours since I saw you pass the new enclosure, and considering how long you had been gone Louisa felt obliged to come and look for you."

And you felt obliged to come with her, thought Verney, who found their thinly-veiled suspicions infuriating.

Louisa had to have her say. "Harriet, it was very wrong of you to play such a trick on your grandmother. As it happens, she is visiting Mrs. Williams

48

at the cottage, so she cannot be aware that you have not yet come in from your drive. Had she been at home, she might have been very much alarmed."

"Oh, do you think so?" replied Harriet, with such an air of innocence that none of the Capels could decide whether she was being ingenuous or impertinent.

Richard had found a gap in the hedge. "I think you may squeeze through here, Harriet. Mrs. Capel will drive you home. And I'll come with you in the curricle, Verney."

These high-handed arrangements left Verney speechless. He was getting ready to say something pretty cutting (though he was not sure what) when it dawned on him that Harriet was behaving with a docility, and indeed a total lack of embarrassment, that was slightly ominous. She seemed to be lost in a happy dream. The locket was apparently forgotten. She joined Louisa in the phaeton, and smiled her thanks to Verney, still clasping the bonnetful of cowslips.

"I never had a pleasanter trip in my life."

The ponies set off at a sharp trot, and the two brothers were left in the lane.

"Well, of all the damned interference!" Verney exploded, as soon as Louisa and Harriet were out of earshot. "Who appointed you the guardians of Harriet's virtue? I suppose you think I brought her out here on purpose to ruin her?"

"Try not to be more of a fool than you can help," said Richard in his most damping manner. "No one has accused you of trying to seduce her. What I want to know is, are you expecting to marry her?"

Verney was taken at a disadvantage. He was ready to swear indignantly—and truthfully—that he had no evil intentions towards Harriet, wouldn't hurt her for the world—but this was something entirely different. He had not yet thought seriously about marrying anyone, and his adventure with Pamela Sutcliffe had left him wary and disenchanted.

"Are you entirely satisfied," continued Richard, "that Harriet Piper is the woman with whom you wish to spend the rest of your life?"

"The rest of my life? Good God, no!"

"Then I suggest you take very good care, or you will find yourself in honour bound to do so."

He began to walk along the road towards the waiting curricle. Verney followed him, sulky and aggrieved.

"I don't see why—"

"Come, my dear fellow! You and I have been at cross-purposes over Harriet since the night you came home. I said some uncharitable things, which I afterwards regretted, yet I don't think my warning was misplaced. The fact is, you are so heedless and unguarded that you are just as liable to get into a scrape with a virtuous young woman as you are with the other sort. It's a different kind of scrape, that's all. You have been amusing yourself with that child, and now she is convinced that you are in love with her."

"I assure you, I've done absolutely nothing—"

"You may have acted with the most rigid propriety, but what does that signify? She would hardly expect anything else, once she decided that you meant to make her an offer of marriage. But I imagine you said and looked and hinted enough to turn her head, poor little creature. You've been flirting with her, and she doesn't know it, she doesn't understand the art of flirtation. What's more, you have made her conspicuous, and people are beginning to talk. If you go on as you are, you will not only end by breaking Harriet's heart, you will also make her an object of public ridicule, which is the lesser injury of the two, I admit—still, it can cause a good deal of distress, especially in a small country society such as ours, where everyone knows everyone else's business far too well. The way a girl has been treated by one man may influence the treatment she receives from others. People are sometimes very cruel."

A few hours earlier Verney might have taken all this with a grain of salt. Since that interlude among the cowslips he felt far less inclined to scoff. He recognised with dismay that Harriet, when she kissed him, had been innocently answering a question he was not prepared to ask. I must have been out of my wits, he thought angrily, flirting with a girl who was too green to know the rules. I'd never have done such a thing if I hadn't left London feeling so wretched, and been made to feel like a criminal in my own home. It was Pamela's fault, Richard's fault. . . . It was his own fault, and he felt ashamed of himself.

"What do you think I should do?" He consulted Richard in a moment of unusual humility.

"Sheer off as gracefully as you can. Don't single her out, in public or in private, and for the present, at any rate, be as formal and distant in your manner as you are able without being uncivil. I'm afraid you will find it disagreeable, but I don't think any other course of action will make your sentiments sufficiently plain. And it will be kinder in the long run."

That made sense, however brutal it sounded. Only a lunatic would marry a girl to avoid hurting her feelings.

Louisa scolded Harriet all the way home, telling her she had been imprudent and unladylike, if not actually fast.

"To leave the carriage and wander off like that, I cannot imagine how you came to do such a thing! You must have known it was wrong! And look at the state you are in, and your bonnet—it's a mercy you were not seen by anyone like Mrs. Wood or Lady Elinor Daly. I knew a girl who lost her reputation because she was caught coming out of a wood with a young man."

Cluck, cluck, thought Harriet, unimpressed. She had a naughty impulse to say that neither she nor her bonnet had been irretrievably ruined, but it was less trouble to abstract her mind and dream blissfully of the moment when Verney would ask her to marry him.

She was rather disappointed, next day, to hear that he had gone off to visit an eccentric uncle on the other side of the county. However, Mr. Henry Capel was always sending for one or other of his nephews to attend his deathbed. His dramatic performances never lasted very long, so Verney was certain to be back for the first of the summer balls at the Southbury Assembly Rooms.

In fact Harriet was less anxious about Verney's going to the ball than she was about her own means of getting there. Mrs. Boyce had made it plain, a year ago, that in her poor health it would be impossible for her to keep late hours and sit in draughts in order to chaperone a dancing granddaughter. It was Mrs. Capel who had generally taken Harriet to balls and parties, a very convenient arrangement until now. All of a sudden the prospect had become extremely awkward. In her present censorious mood Mrs. Theo would spoil everything. Luckily there was an alternative. Harriet would spend the night with her particular friend Sukey Wood, who lived on the outskirts of Southbury.

She was therefore delighted, the following day, to see the Woods' chaise drive through the lodge gates and make the circuit of Church Green. The coachman drew up, not at the Dower House, but in front of Bell Cottage. Mrs. Wood was paying a morning call on the new arrivals, and Sukey was with her.

After a few minutes' cogitation Harriet also presented herself at Bell Cottage and asked whether Miss Johnson was at home. As Miss Johnson and her guests were clearly visible through the window, the answer was bound to be yes, and she was promptly shown into the small, elegant drawing room.

She had the grace to feel a little uncomfortable. She could hardly say that she simply wanted a word with Sukey—perhaps it would be better if she pretended not to have known that Miss Johnson had callers? She was getting ready to look surprised when she realised, jut in time, that the Woods' carriage was standing in the drive outside, plain for all to see.

This was the kind of absurd social dilemma that was always overshadowing poor Harriet's efforts to behave like a grown-up young lady. She stood stammering on the threshold.

"Do come in, my dear Miss Harriet," Julia Johnson greeted her. "You know everybody here, and I'm sure your ears must be burning, for I have just been telling Miss Susan Wood how kind you have been in showing us so many beautiful walks."

Harriet found herself established beside Sukey on the sofa, able to look about and admire the charming setting that Miss Johnson had created for herself in such a short time: the amber silk curtains looped back from the windows, the Swansea flowerpots on top of the book-laden chiffonier, the rosewood worktable and, of course, the harp. The beautiful Julia was very much the mistress of her surroundings and perfectly able to converse with Mrs. Wood, who was a formidable country lady with a sound knowledge of her own world, though not setting out to be fashionable.

The maid brought in a silver tray, and while they were all being offered a glass of wine with a slice of cake, Harriet was able to whisper to Sukey, "I've such a lot of news for you."

"Tell me all!" demanded Sukey, who had encouraged Harriet to fall in love with Verney Capel and felt personally involved. She was enthralled by the latest developments, and quite saw why her friend did not wish to go to the ball with Mrs. Theo Capel.

"Even supposing she offers to take me," added Harriet, "and I dare say she won't, after my little adventure among the cowslips, she has such antique notions."

"Oh yes, she is the sort of person who thinks it improper to dance more than twice with the same partner. You would find that very inconvenient! I am sure Mama would let you come with us, only where are you to sleep? We have no spare room at present, you know—the wing is full up with the children having measles."

Harriet had forgotten this domestic catastrophe. "They have been having the measles for ever! Surely they must have finished by now?"

"Edwin has got them very badly. And Mama is anxious that Selina shan't catch them, because of her always being sickly, so she has my bed, and I am sleeping in Mama's dressing room, which is dreadfully uncomfortable. I have nowhere to put my things and no privacy for writing my journal."

"Then what am I to do?"

"Wouldn't they let you drive home alone after the ball? In your grandfather's carriage, with the coachman and footman to look after you?"

Harriet shook her head. Southbury was five miles from Wardley. They would never let her drive all that way, late at night, without a female companion. An idea struck her.

"Are you going to the ball, Miss Johnson?"

Her hostess was rather taken aback. "To the ball? Oh no, we never thought of such a thing."

"But you would like to go, would you not? I am persuaded you would enjoy it. If it is a question of the distance—I know you don't keep a carriage —my grandfather would be very pleased for you and Mrs. Williams to make use of ours."

"That is extremely civil of your grandfather," said Mrs. Williams drily. "I wonder what he will say when you tell him."

"Wait a minute," said Miss Johnson, before Harriet had time to answer. "It is not just a question of the carriage. We are in no position to attend this ball. It is quite an exclusive affair, is it not? With tickets available to regular patrons only? We should be turned back at the door."

"But Mrs. Wood can get tickets for you," protested Harriet. "Can't you, ma'am?"

As soon as the words were out she knew that she had made a fearful blunder, practically forcing Mrs. Wood to sponsor two ladies she had met for the first time twenty minutes ago. She glanced guiltily at Sukey's mother, who gave her an admonishing frown but took her cue with well-bred facility.

"I shall be delighted to procure tickets for you. Nothing will give me greater pleasure."

"You are too kind, ma'am," said Miss Johnson, who had flushed with embarrassment, "but I assure you there is not the smallest need—Mrs. Williams and I came here intending to live very quietly: we do not expect to go to balls—"

An amiable struggle now took place, Mrs. Wood insisting that they should accept her offer of tickets, while Mrs. Williams and Miss Johnson protested that they could not impose on her. Harriet considered it a great waste of time. She was sure that Julia Johnson must want to go to Southbury, in spite of her protests, and that she would be an immediate success when she got there.

And sure enough, when the great evening arrived, Harriet entered the Assembly Rooms in a high state of anticipation, accompanied by Julia and Mrs. Williams.

She had not seen Verney since his return, but she knew he was home. She was wearing a new dress in his honour: white figured muslin, garlanded with tiny rosebuds at the neck and waist. Her hair had been specially cropped and she knew she was looking her best—even though she also knew herself outshone by her companion. Julia wore a dove-grey gauze tunic over a lilac satin slip, unusual colours which drew attention to the fact that she was older than most of the other young ladies, and actually managed to turn this into an advantage. Her hair was dressed in the Greek style, pinned up and falling in tendrils from the back of her head. Her eyes were like grey stars under their dark lashes. Har-

56

riet was sure that no one so entrancing had ever been seen in the Southbury ballroom. Quietly as she stepped into the gathering of strangers, she seemed to radiate light.

Mrs. Wood was there, ready to introduce Mrs. Williams and Miss Johnson to the people they ought to meet. Harriet already knew all the local gentry who came to these balls. Verney had not yet arrived, and she was not in the mood to be interested by anyone else. The chaperones clustered in their favourite corner, manoeuvring for the best chairs, while the young ladies sauntered up and down in front of them, pretending to be absorbed in their own conversations, never looking at the young men who hung about outside the cardroom, as though they had not the faintest intention of dancing with anyone. It was eight o'clock on a fine May evening, but the shutters were tightly closed, and the room was lit by two great chandeliers, each giving off a great glow of warmth which would soon be very oppressive. The orchestra was tuning up. The wheedle of fiddles and the smell of hot wax—this brought back the half-fearful excitement at the beginning of every ball. Harriet glanced towards the door.

"Some of your partners have still to arrive?" hazarded Julia.

"Yes. That is—have you met Verney Capel? Sir Richard's youngest brother?"

"He was at the Parsonage when we dined there last week."

"So you are acquainted with the Capels, Miss Johnson," remarked Amelia Porter, a young woman with a keen sense of her own importance. "You are fortunate. They do not visit newcomers as a rule."

"Sir Richard Capel is my landlord. He has been very kind—"

"Oh, that explains it. He is exceedingly affable to all his tenants, great and small. But you will not see him here this evening. He never comes, has not attended a single assembly since poor Lady Capel was first taken ill, about six years ago."

"Indeed?" said Julia. "How very odd. He has just come through the door."

Miss Porter turned and stared, not at all pleased at being made to appear foolish. And it was perfectly true that Sir Richard had stopped coming to the assemblies once his wife was no longer well enough to come with him. His reentry into society was something of a landmark, and there was a murmur of pleased speculation as the three tall brothers crossed the floor together. Louisa was beside her husband, alert and pretty, very pleased with her menfolk.

Almost every feminine eye was on Sir Richard. That splendid profile, the raven-black hair, the history of solitary grief: he possessed all the qualities most likely to inspire romantic devotion. Harriet was thinking how well Verney looked in knee-breeches.

"What a covey of Capels," she exclaimed, intercepting him neatly as they reached the top of the room. "Did you have a very tiresome visit? I am so glad you managed to get away."

"It was not at all difficult," said Verney, a little repressively. "How do you do, Miss Johnson."

"But your uncle," persisted Harriet, hardly giving Julia time to answer. "I thought he was always so uncommonly cross. I thought—" She saw that Verney was not responding to her bubbling high spirits, realised she was talking too much, and fell silent.

The younger men were coming over now in twos and threes to join the throng of girls. Sir Richard and Theo were talking to old Admiral Porter. Verney glanced round at them, and it suddenly struck Harriet that if neither of his brothers was dancing, he and his partner would have the privilege of opening the ball. Absolute happiness was about to begin.

"May I have the honour?" asked Verney formally. And offered his arm to Julia.

She placed her narrow, gloved hand on his sleeve, and they moved off together.

Harriet was left gazing after them, dumb with chagrin. She saw them go right up to the top of the set and speak to the leader of the orchestra, for of course Julia would call the tune—choose the music for the first dance. Everyone was watching her and Verney as they stood there, so happy and smiling.

A partner presented himself at Harriet's elbow: she accepted him, and only then noticed that he was Mr. Arthur Slingsby, the dullest man in the neighbourhood, and she was saddled with him for two whole dances.

"I have not had the pleasure of seeing you since the last of our regular winter assemblies," said Mr. Slingsby. "Do you not think these new summer meetings are an excellent innovation? Winter is generally considered the season for balls, yet this seems to me a very singular circumstance, when one reflects on the many varieties of inclement weather to which our country is prone. For one cannot deny that mud and rain are as objectionable in their way as frost and snow."

"No, of course not," said Harriet. "I mean, yes." As soon as they started dancing she began to feel

59

more cheerful. The lilt of the music was so be-
guiling and the gaiety so infectious. She saw the
eager faces and the girls' pale dresses, the light leaping on pearls and spangles; she surrendered to the
enjoyment of weaving and turning through a complicated figure, and the rush of golden air. . . . It
was right that Verney should have asked Miss Johnson to open the ball: an older woman making her
first appearance in a strange neighbourhood. He'll
ask me next, thought Harriet, with renewed confidence.

But when the time for changing partners came,
Verney was engaged to dance with Maria Daly, the
handsome Irish wife of his friend Tom Daly, the
master of foxhounds. Harriet had to make do with
Amelia Porter's brother, a very respectable young
clergyman.

Julia had now acquired a court of admirers; she
was certainly the prettiest woman in the room. Sukey Wood made a grimace at Harriet, which meant,
why aren't you dancing with Verney? Harriet pretended not to notice. The chaperones watched everyone from their perches by the wall. Most of the
older men had retreated into the cardroom. Sir
Richard was still standing at the top of the room,
gazing straight down the double rank of dancers
with an abstracted expression. If he wasn't going
to dance or play whist it was difficult to see why
he had come.

When they got to the third pair of dances, Harriet cunningly stationed herself beside Verney while
he was talking to a friend. Presently the other
young man moved away, and they were left alone.

"Oh—Harriet!" He spoke abruptly, with a curious
awkwardness, and said nothing more.

A new set was forming in the middle of the floor,

but Harriet and Verney were isolated and immovable.

"Well, are you going to ask me to dance?" she enquired rather snappishly. "Or have you lost your tongue?"

"If you don't learn to mend your manners, my girl," said Verney, "no one will ask you to dance."

For the first instant she thought he was teasing her, and then realised that he was quite serious.

"You must not hold up your partners at pistol point. Men don't like a girl to be possessive, even in jest."

Was he calling her a man-hunter? It was a brutal snub. She stood stock-still, too distressed to answer.

"Come along," he said more moderately. "The music's beginning. There's no call to look so downcast; I was simply giving you a hint."

"If you don't want to dance with me—"

"Oh, don't be missish, Harriet!" he exclaimed, taking her arm.

As he led her out, an extraordinary event took place in front of them. Julia had been talking to Mrs. Williams and some of the older ladies. As soon as she turned round she was pounced on by two watchful gentlemen, each hoping to secure her as a partner, but before either had a chance to speak, Sir Richard, abandoning his Olympian detachment walked straight up to her, and asked: "Will you give me the great pleasure of dancing with you, Miss Johnson, if you please?"

Even in her present state of confusion and hurt feelings, Harriet knew that this was very extraordinary. Perhaps Julia herself was the only person in the room who was not at all surprised: she could hardly be expected to appreciate how unusual it was for Sir Richard to pay any young woman such a distinguishing compliment. She accepted gracefully, and they took their places towards the bottom of the set immediately next to Harriet and Verney.

Amelia Porter, a little further up, was craning her neck to see them.

"You must admit she was right," whispered Julia to Harriet. "He is an exemplary landlord."

"What's that you are saying?" demanded Sir Richard.

"I was merely telling Miss Piper how well you live up to your reputation, sir." Julia gazed up at him, too beautiful and too serene to seem in the least impertinent. "We were informed this evening that you are exceedingly affable to all your tenants, great and small."

"And in which category do you place yourself, ma'am?" he enquired immediately.

Verney laughed. Julia, glancing at him, said: "I am afraid your brother measures out his affability by the square foot, Mr. Capel. How many acres should I have to rent before he asked me to dance a minuet?"

This amused Verney even more. Richard was watching Julia with an expression of wonder and delight: he looked suddenly ten years younger.

They were still working their way up the set and had nothing to do in the dance. Both the brothers continued to make much of Julia, flirting with her in a half-serious, half-satirical manner. Harriet, the only silent member of the quartet looked from one to the other, puzzled and a little forlorn. She felt that something was happening which she could not understand. Julia tried to draw her into the conversation, and Sir Richard reminded Verney rather acidly that he had a partner of his own.

At that moment the tide of music reached them,

and they were swept into the waves and cross-currents of the dance. In their second passage up the set Verney did talk quite a lot to Harriet, but when their two dances were over, he returned her to Mrs. Williams, made a slight bow, and walked away.

The rest of the evening was like a bad dream. It was hot and noisy; she hardly heard or cared what people were saying to her. How stupid and tawdry they all looked, bobbing up and down and sweating. Her new shoes pinched, and she decided she would just as soon go and sit in a corner—until she realised that she might be forced to do so, whether she liked it or not. She was having some difficulty in getting partners. There was a perfectly logical reason for this: her most useful acquaintances at the Southbury Assemblies were Sukey Wood's three brothers, and Sukey had warned them to stay away from Harriet tonight, because she had other fish to fry. If Harriet had worked this out, she would have been extremely annoyed with her interfering friend, but she was already too upset to think sensibly, and gradually became convinced that Verney was right: she had made herself conspicuous as a man-hunter and was therefore to be avoided.

In the last dance before supper she was again obliged to stand up with Mr. Slingsby, that complete zero. When it was over she escaped from him, murmuring something about her chaperone, and then saw that Mrs. Williams had already been joined by Julia, and that Verney was escorting them both.

It was more than she could bear. She was nearly crying with humiliation, headache and disappointment, and she did not know where to go or what to do with herself. She was rescued from this painful situation by Mrs. Theo Capel, who had noticed pretty well everything that was going on.

"Come and sit with us, my dear Harriet," she said in her bracing way. "Theo, find us a comfortable corner, if you can." And she propelled Harriet past the card players into the tearoom beyond.

When they sat down, she managed things so that Harriet was at the end of the table next to the wall, where she could recover her composure without having to join in the general chatter.

Julia was at a nearby table, between Verney and Richard, who had come into the tearoom with Tom and Maria Daly. They were all now together in an animated group. Julia seemed to be holding a conversational balance between Verney and his brother. She still looked refreshingly cool in her grey gauze tunic with the submerged gleam of lilac.

"She is a showy young woman," remarked Louisa. "I can't say I care for her."

"Don't you, ma'am? She is very charming."

"A little too charming perhaps. A single woman, in a circle where she is quite unknown—what business has she to be so easy in her manner? However, I dare say she will know how to deal with Verney."

Harriet folded her slice of bread-and-butter. "Is he—do you think Verney is falling in love with Miss Johnson?"

"My dear child, Verney has never been *in love* in the whole course of his life. He is merely willing to amuse himself with any female who takes his fancy. I am afraid he has not yet learnt his lesson, in spite of what happened in London."

"What was it that happened in London?"

"He got into a scrape with a married woman and had to send in his papers. But that is not a subject for your ears," said Louisa, recollecting herself. "I am sorry I mentioned it."

All Harriet's hopes were finally dashed. She had come to the ball thinking Verney was in love with her, and it had therefore seemed incredible that he should have changed his mind so abruptly. But if he had never loved her, if she was simply one of his procession of flirts, it was only too natural that he should abandon her for the fascinating Julia.

8

"You have not forgotten," said Mrs. Boyce to her husband, "that Sir Richard has invited us to drink tea beside the lake."

The General had forgotten, and was not at all pleased to be reminded. "What the devil does Capel want to give a damned tea party for? And if he must do such a deuced odd thing, why don't he do it at the Hall? I've no fancy to sit in that sham castle of his, getting bitten to death by a pack of midges."

"Lady Adela's Bower was built as a tea pavilion. I remember Lady Capel holding a rout there some years ago. I dare say he means to revive the custom."

"He's not holding a rout this evening?" asked the General in alarm.

"Nothing of the sort. It is just ourselves, the Theo Capels, and the ladies from Bell Cottage."

He brightened a little, exclaiming that Miss Johnson was a fine young woman, and a pretty-behaved one too; she always had time to spare for an old fellow who'd been put out to grass, in spite of all the beaux that were dangling after her. "And

I tell you what, miss," he added, catching sight of his granddaughter as she slumped in her chair with a white, listless face, "you could take a leaf from Miss Johnson's book. It's a pity all young females ain't as pleasant and obliging as she is."

"I am well aware of Miss Johnson's perfection, Grandpapa," said Harriet in a stifled voice. Shortly afterwards she left the room.

"What's the matter with her?" the old man asked his wife. "Not crossed in love, is she?"

"My dear General, what will you think of next? She's hardly out of the schoolroom. Time enough to fall in love when she goes to join Hetty in Ireland."

Mrs. Boyce always shut her eyes to anything unpleasant, and she had an equally priceless gift for inventing circumstances that made her feel more comfortable, such as the hopeful fiction that her daughter would eventually take charge of Harriet.

Harriet knew better. She knew that her mother did not want her, any more than Verney did. She would have been thankful, just now, to get away from Wardley and join her family in Ireland, but there was no chance of that; she would just have to stay here, where she was so miserable, and where everyone knew she had thrown herself at Verney and been rejected. If only she had not boasted to Sukey Wood—who had gone round gossiping to half the neighbourhood about poor Harriet's disappointment. She would still have had a broken heart, but it wouldn't have been quite so humiliating.

There must be something wrong with me, she thought, standing in the middle of her bedroom and staring at herself in the looking glass. I don't know what it is, I'm not ugly, but no one can love me and I suppose no one ever will.

That evening after dinner, as Harriet and her

grandparents set out from the Dower House, they met the Theo Capels, also bound for the tea party.

"I see we are all in good time," said Louisa. She glanced back at the closed door of Bell Cottage, and said with a faint satisfaction, "No sign yet of Miss Johnson and her friend."

As they walked along the drive, the General asked the Rector, accusingly, what his brother meant by giving a tea party.

"I believe it is intended as a mark of civility towards his new tenants, sir. He felt it would be awkward to be giving a dinner party for two ladies, and this seemed a good alternative."

"There was no need for him to entertain them at all," remarked Louisa. "We asked them to dinner and one did everything that was proper."

They left the drive and began to walk downhill through a grove of trees. They were entering the pleasure gardens from the south, the opposite side to the Hall, and everything was in reverse. They saw the lake ahead of them, the Rustic Bridge, and Lady Adela's Bower on the far bank, every little pointed tower tipped with rosy lights from the westering sun. A table with a white cloth had been set up in the pavilion; Kitty and Chloe were arranging cups and saucers, assisted by Miss Pringle and a footman. Various iron seats were drawn up to the table, and an elderly lady was sitting on one of them. It was Mrs. Williams, and she was looking at a group of people on the bridge. Eight-year-old Ned Capel was perched astride the stone balustrade, with his father standing next to him. Verney was a little further on. Between the two men, the focus of their complete attention, Julia was doing something complicated with a folded sheet of paper.

Apparently the tenants of Bell Cottage had stolen a march on their neighbours.

"Well!" said Louisa in a burst of indignation.

A few moments later she was saying to Richard: "I am sorry we mistook the arrangement. I distinctly understood that you did not expect us until seven—"

"My dear Louisa, it's of no consequence," said Richard blandly. "Do sit still, Ned, or you'll fall in the lake."

His delicate younger son was small and slight, with fair, almost transparent features. He was inclined to get overexcited.

"I hope that child won't take a chill off the water," said Louisa. "I didn't know he was to be included in the party. It's high time he was in bed." She thought Richard must have taken leave of his senses.

He did not seem to hear her, his whole attention was fixed on Julia.,

"Miss Johnson is showing us a new way to make paper boats," Ned informed his aunt. "She's done a whole fleet of them."

"Wait till this one is ready, and then we'll have a race," said Julia, turning her triangle of paper inside out and tweaking up the sails.

She soon had Ned and his father and Verney dropping boats off the bridge and running to the other side to see them come through. Harriet and her grandfather and Theo were all drawn into this childish sport. Mrs. Boyce had gone to join Mrs. Williams. Louisa stood by herself, smiling carefully to show she was not annoyed.

"Do you remember making a model of the Victory, Verney?" asked Harriet, gazing mournfully at him with her large brown eyes.

"It was a very bad model," said Verney, in a snubbing voice.

He was annoyed with her for addressing him in that beseeching tone, for being such a spaniel. Moving abruptly away from her, he saw Julia picking up an Indian cotton shawl which she had hung carelessly over the iron trellis work of the Rustic Bridge. One of the threads had caught on a jagged edge of rusticity, and she was trying to work it free.

"Let me help you," he offered, reaching across, so that his hand lay warm and sentient beside her own. It was a purely accidental contact, but she snatched her arm back as though she had been stung.

"Please don't trouble yourself! I can manage."

"I beg your pardon," said Verney stiffly.

But she was not listening, her glance went flying past him to Richard, who was talking to Ned.

He turned to her, smiling. "Is anything wrong?"

"My silly shawl, Sir Richard . . ." said Julia with a sort of rueful sweetness which sounded to Verney quite artificial, a parody of her usual manner. And her eyes had a calculating expression which reminded him of the eyes of his mistress Pamela Sutcliffe, that angelic liar, when she was beginning one of her acts.

Richard released the shawl, and was allowed to place it reverently round Julia's shoulders, just as they were called into the pavilion for tea.

As they clustered round the table, Verney conducted a little experiment. He went and stood close to Julia, as though meaning to sit beside her. Julia immediately decided she did not like that end of the table and insinuated herself into a chair between Richard and old General Boyce.

This was exactly what Verney had expected. Flirting very lightly with her at the Southbury Ball (chiefly in order to discourage Harriet) he had been surprised and rather piqued to find himself cut out by Richard. It was so ludicrous—Richard was thirty-seven, and for the whole of Verney's grown-up life he had been out of commission—Catherine's devoted husband, and then Catherine's grief-stricken widower. Of course he ought not to grieve for ever, and he was so extremely handsome that only a coxcomb (Verney assured himself) would mind being put in the shade by such a brother. What he resented was the fact that no ordinary rivalry existed. In her badly concealed attempt to catch a rich husband Julia was determined that no one else should waste her time, spoil her opportunities, or behave towards her in any way that an observer might misinterpret—and he resented this, not on his own account but on Richard's. However charmingly she stage-managed it, such a single-minded pursuit could only be repulsive.

She's even wooing the children, he thought cynically, hearing her say: "What pretty china."

"Do you think so?" Kitty was visibly pleased. "We painted it ourselves, and Papa sent it back to the factory to be glazed. It is not quite perfect, I'm afraid. You could not compare it with Royal Worcester."

"But Royal Wardley is so much more original."

The children were delighted with this. She knew exactly how to win their confidence. Paper boats and painted china—if Dick wasn't away at school she'd probably be playing cricket!

Mrs. Williams asked the history of Lady Adela's Bower, and in the course of a discussion that followed, Chloe said she wished her Papa would build another folly; couldn't Miss Johnson persuade him?

70

How will she deal with that, Verney wondered. If she tries too hard at this juncture, she will seem forward and pushing, but if she disclaims any influence over Papa she will run the risk of looking coy, as well as insincere.

Julia avoided both these pitfalls by saying, "I believe your Papa will leave a more valuable record of his stewardship. I dare say a field of corn is not so romantic as a ruined tower, yet the achievement of growing more food, feeding more people on this beleaguered island, surely that is something to be proud of?"

Bravo, thought Verney. You couldn't have done better.

It was true that Richard had plunged all his energy and intelligence, and a good deal of his money, into the cause of farming and land improvement. He still represented Southbury in Parliament; it was a family borough which he had held since he was twenty-one, attending the House as a Pittite Tory, deeply concerned with the abolition of the slave trade, Catholic emancipation, and the effective prosecution of the war. Now Pitt was dead, the war dragged on, but the change in Richard's perspective had a more personal origin: Catherine's long illness. His affectionate care for her had kept him tied down here in the country; he had taken up farming seriously, and was now a leading authority.

Julia had evidently become aware of this. She was asking about merino sheep, and her questions were a little too knowledgeable to ring quite true.

"Good God!" said Verney. "A lady who reads the Agricultural Reports—shall we never get to the end of your accomplishments, Miss Johnson? Such industry—and such foresight!"

71

"And what is that supposed to mean?" demanded Richard angrily.

"It was a compliment. I am sure Miss Johnson understands me very well."

Julia was flushed, and her remarkable poise had deserted her. She certainly understood Verney only too well, and had nothing more to say on the subject of agriculture.

"Can I feed the ducks?" asked Ned.

They collected a plate of crumbs, and he scattered them on the water for a colony of mallards and their chicks who came round bobbing and diving for their supper. After which he and his sisters said good night to the company and went back to the house with Miss Pringle. The Boyces and Mrs. Williams decided to sit a little longer in the pavilion while the six remaining members of the party went for a stroll through the pleasure gardens.

They stuck together in an awkward little procession. Louisa and Verney were both unwilling to let Julia walk with Richard alone; the Rector remained with his wife, and Harriet was forced to go along with them. She was feeling wretchedly unhappy. She had hardly spoken since her one bid for notice had irritated Verney at the bridge. She had been spared the pain of watching him carry on a triumphant flirtation with Julia, but she did not really enjoy seeing him sulk and behave badly because he had been ousted by his elder brother.

The beautiful softness of dusk had begun to smudge the outlines of the trees. All the greens of the garden floated together into the colour of shadows. The surface of the lake took on a milky sheen like mother of pearl. Up and down the little paths they went, admiring the prospects of the Nunnery, the Grotto, the Cascade. And all the way Richard talked quietly and seriously to Julia. Verney interrupted and made acid comments. And Julia ignored Verney and listened attentively to Richard.

9

The heavy door of the library slid silently open.

"Good afternoon, Verney," said Louisa. "I hoped I might find you here."

Verney got to his feet, resentfully. He had been comfortably drowsing over the *Quarterly Review*, and he had no wish to be disturbed by Louisa, who probably wanted to lecture him about Harriet. His conscience was nagging him quite enough already, he knew he had treated the poor girl very badly, but there was no reason why he should listen to sermons from Louisa.

"I dare say you would prefer to see Richard," he said, and added cunningly, by way of a distraction, "He has driven Miss Johnson and Mrs. Williams over to Southbury."

"Yes, I know. It is on that subject I wish to consult you."

"Oh," said Verney, setting a chair for her with much more alacrity.

"I am becoming increasingly anxious." Louisa fixed him with her bright blue gaze. "Richard appears to be— Well, I'm afraid I must use the word—infatuated with that young woman."

"Yes, I agree. I could hardly believe it at first: Richard has always been so extremely reserved, never looked twice at any woman but Catherine. I suppose that's the answer, he's been too solitary for too long."

"Shutting himself up and meeting no one," amplified Louisa, though in fact she had rather encouraged this isolation. "With the result that he has now fallen a victim to a scheming adventuress—"

"Isn't that rather a strong term? A scheming husband-hunter, if you like, but Julia Johnson is perfectly respectable, not at all the sort of vulgar creature who haunts the public rooms at every smart watering place. That is what most people mean by an adventuress."

"I am sure," said Louisa tartly, "that you know the species much better than I do, my dear Verney."

Verney grinned. You could trust Louisa to score a point there. All the same, he was interested in her choice of words, for he was by now deeply suspicious of Julia. Plenty of girls had tried to make up to Richard, but none of them had acted their parts as hard and as consistently as this one. She was very good, he would have been taken in himself, but for her occasional giveaway moments of affectation, and the extremely guarded expression that sometimes came into her eyes. . . .

"Why did you call her an adventuress?" he asked abruptly.

"Because I think she's here under false colours. I don't believe she was recommended by Captain Bowyer, or that their mothers were ever at school together!"

This was far more dramatic than he had expected. "Whatever gave you that idea?"

She was eager to explain. She had been convinced all along that there was something strange about Julia Johnson's antecedents (though she did not say why) and during the past fortnight she had set out to ask both Julia and Mrs. Williams a great

74

many questions about their supposed acquaintance with the Bowyer family. Very soon they had not only contradicted each other, each had contradicted her own previous statements. They did actually know the maiden name of Captain Bowyer's mother—she had been a Miss Sayer from Lincolnshire—but all other details were confused, the fragments of a story that had not been sufficiently rehearsed.

"They must know George Bowyer at least."

"Well enough to know that he is in the West Indies and can't easily be got at. They were able to take his name in vain."

"Yes, but Louisa, why? Why should they wish to come and bury themselves at Wardley?"

That was a puzzle in itself, however you looked at it.

"You aren't going to tell me that Miss Johnson came here on the off chance of captivating Richard?" he enquired ironically.

"No, certainly not. That would be absurd."

"Then what other reason, what possible attraction—"

"I think she is running away from a scandal. No, listen to me, Verney: don't interrupt. She is very reluctant to answer questions, as though there is something she is determined to hide at all costs. As though she has a guilty secret. Suppose she has lost her character in her own neighbourhood, was obliged to leave the district. She has one friend who is in her confidence. They go to London, where they meet George Bowyer, and learn just enough about him to get themselves accepted as tenants of Bell Cottage by means of a trick. Oh, I grant you it sounds a desperate venture, but consider how much it would do to restore Julia Johnson's credit. She has only to stay here a few months, and then she can pass anywhere as a young lady from Wilshire, a friend of the Capels of Wardley. And that is no mean recommendation."

"You think that's why she came?"

"I think it's why she came, but once she'd met Richard I believe she changed her plan. She means to marry him if she can, and you will have to put him on his guard."

"I?" said Verney, thunderstruck. "You must be mad. He wouldn't listen to me. If anyone tackles him, it ought to be Theo."

"Theo won't interfere. He's very obstinate at times."

"Then you yourself, Louisa. Richard has a great admiration for you and I'm sure he would respect your opinion."

Looking rather confused, Louisa said she could not possibly discuss Julia's past with Richard, it would be too indelicate.

"I don't see why. You're discussing it with me."

Louisa glared at him and said nothing. Verney decided that Theo had made her promise that she wouldn't interfere either. Presumably it had not occurred to him that she might enlist an ally to do her interfering for her.

"I shall write to Coverdale," she was saying. Coverdale was the Capel family lawyer and a man of business, who had drawn up the lease of Bell Cottage. "I shall ask him how Miss Johnson first approached him, whether she brought some sort of introduction from Captain Bowyer, and so forth. I shall also ask him to find out all he can concerning her true history. In the meantime I wish you would persuade Richard not to commit himself too far. You could at least give him a hint."

It was exactly like Louisa, reflected Verney, several hours later: she thoroughly disapproved of him,

76

and often said so, yet she was still capable of singling him out as a suitable person to drop hints to the head of the family.

He was alone with Richard for the first time since this embarrassing duty had been suggested to him. Dinner was over; Miss Pringle and the girls had withdrawn, leaving the men to enjoy their wine. Richard sat at the head of the table: behind him on the wall was that painting by Claude with the dark slender trees and the distant water, so oddly reminiscent of the Wardley pleasure gardens. Richard was looking happier than Verney had seen him for years. He must have been very lonely, he deserved a change of fortune. Which was all the more reason why he must be protected from Julia Johnson and her snares.

"Give the port a fair wind, if you please."

"What? Oh, I beg your pardon." Verney pushed the decanter in its silver coaster towards his brother, taking care to rotate it in a clockwise direction. To send the port the wrong way round the table brought bad luck. "Did you meet anyone in Southbury?"

"I saw Oliver Porter; and Mrs. Wood with several of her daughters."

"I dare say they were a little surprised."

"Surprised to see me in Southbury High Street? Why should they be?"

"To see you with Miss Johnson," said Verney with considerable temerity.

"What's so extraordinary in that? You are frequently seen driving ladies around the countryside."

"Yes, but you aren't."

"This seems a very good time to begin."

"Do you think you've been altogether wise in your choice of a companion?"

77

"What have you against my companion?" asked Richard sharply.

Verney did not know what to say.

"Well, I suppose there is no need to enquire," remarked his brother in a cold, hard voice. "You have displayed the most ill-judged and ill-bred antagonism towards Julia—Miss Johnson—ever since she made it plain that she did not care for your kind of gallantry. I have felt thoroughly ashamed of you once or twice, and I would have told you so before, only she particularly desired me not to do so."

Verney sat stiffly, fingering his glass, and staring at the massive silver ornament, representing the Triumph of Bacchus, whose chariots and satyrs rioted decorously across the polished table. Richard's attack had made him very indignant but he did not answer at once, because another part of his mind had received a warning message. If Richard and Julia could discuss his attitude so freely, the affair must have progressed a good deal further than he had supposed. It was distinctly ominous that Richard had used her Christian name.

Perhaps Richard felt that his own position was ambiguous, for he said, in a voice that was not entirely free from bravado, "I may as well tell you that I am going to marry Julia Johnson."

"You've already made her an offer?"

Richard hesitated. "I mean to marry her if she'll have me."

"Oh, she'll have you, never fear."

"I find your tone extremely offensive. And what business is it of yours, whom I marry?"

"Your happiness is bound to be a matter of concern to your whole family."

"Indeed? Then why aren't they all here in a deputation? Or perhaps you have been chosen as their spokesman?"

"Not precisely," admitted Verney, feeling unable to implicate Louisa, but cursing her from the bottom of his heart.

"You are too imprecise altogether. Give me one sound and definite reason why you dislike Julia."

"I don't dislike her," said Verney uneasily. "But I find her so very—well, you've only known her five weeks; you know nothing whatever of her past life, where she comes from—"

"This is absurd. I can tell from my own observation that she is a young woman of birth and character, and if that isn't enough to satisfy you, she was recommended to Coverdale by George Bowyer—"

"Was she? Are you sure? I believe she has contradicted herself continually on this subject, and is hardly able to tell the same story two days running."

"My God, I've put up with enough of your impudence!" exclaimed Richard, suddenly becoming very angry indeed. "How dare you spy on my future wife? How dare you speak of her as though she was a dishonest servant with forged references! I would not have believed it possible—but the fact is, the degradation of your mind betrays you at every turn. You seduce the wives of your friends, play fast and loose with silly schoolgirls; I suppose it's no wonder that you cannot meet an unprotected woman without making her the object of some filthy calumny—"

"I never heard so many damned lies!" burst out Verney, infuriated by this gloss on his recent activities. "If you must know, I was once seduced by the wife of one of my friends—yes, she seduced me, and if it's ungentlemanly to say so, I don't care. I was completely deceived. Behind all her modesty and morality and her fine-lady airs, Pamela was an insatiable trollop, and it will serve you right if your precious Julia is no better—"

He knew he had gone too far, but he had no time to retract. Richard was standing over him, pale and menacing; had gripped him by the shoulders and dragged him out of his chair. Then he was being shaken like a rag doll, the darkness thundered in his brain, as he clutched feebly at Richard's wrists and gasped for air.

Richard flung him against the table. The Triumph of Bacchus tipped off its plinth and crashed on to the ground.

The old butler came hurrying in with cries of alarm.

"Sir Richard! Master Verney! What's amiss?" He had known them since they were boys.

"Go away, Smethurst," said Richard.

"But sir—"

"You heard what I said."

Smethurst retreated, making gloomy mutterings about what their poor father would have said. (A proper gentleman, he was.)

Richard had always been considered a paladin among proper gentlemen. He did not look it this evening; his black hair disarranged, his collar awry and a frightening glitter in his eyes.

Verney sat down, rather shakily, massaging his throat.

"I am sorry," he ventured, after a short silence. "I did not mean to imply—what you thought. You mistook my meaning."

His apology was not accepted.

"You have an hour to pack and go." Richard's voice was husky, almost unrecognisable. "If I find you still here at eight o'clock, I shall personally throw you out of the house."

He left the room without once looking in Verney's direction.

Verney remained staring in an unfocused way at the overturned silver. He was angry, miserable, and above all stunned. He would not have thought it possible that he and Richard could quarrel so bitterly, and all on account of that damned woman. He helped himself to a glass of brandy and tried to face the fact that he had been turned out of his own home. Where was he going to spend the night? He could go to the Parsonage, Theo would take him in, but he would then be at uncomfortably close quarters to two people he wanted to avoid. Not only Julia but Harriet. He would do better to take refuge with Tom and Maria Daly.

As he made his plans with a dull inevitability, he was haunted by the memory of Richard, white with passion, violent and unforgiving, a Richard whose existence he had never suspected until today. This was the high-minded lover, the fanatical idealist, defending the goddess in whom he could not allow the smallest imperfection. Did Julia know what a dangerous spirit she had uncaged? And what was Julia herself? An ambitious husband-hunter, nothing worse? Or could it be true that she was hiding a disgraceful secret? In which case, he thought, God help her if Richard ever finds out.

PART TWO

After the Wedding

1

SIR RICHARD CAPEL and Miss Julia Johnson were married by special licence in Wardley Parish Church on the sixteenth of June. It was a very quiet wedding. The Rector conducted the service with his usual grave sincerity. The bridegroom's daughters sat beaming in the family pew, one each side of their outraged Aunt Louisa, who endured the wretched business with a face of stone. The bride was an orphan with no close relations; the only witness on her side was Mrs. Williams.

Verney was not at the wedding. He had left the district, and no one knew where he had gone.

Sir Richard and the new Lady Capel took a short wedding tour to Weymouth, and by the time they returned, Bell Cottage was empty once again. They had invited Mrs. Williams to make her home there, but she preferred to return to Cheshire.

General and Mrs. Boyce were also preparing to make a move; they were going to stay with Mrs. Boyce's unmarried brothers in Dorset. This was an annual event. They never took Harriet with them to Gossington, and she usually spent July and August with the Woods, but this year she had not been asked. Sukey was off to join some cousins at Ramsgate.

"And if the truth be told," said Louisa to her husband, "I dare say Mrs. Wood manoeuvred the Ramsgate visit in order to prevent Sukey and Harriet being thrown together for weeks on end—two silly girls idling away their time and talking of nothing but love! It would do Harriet far more good to come here and profit by a little rational society. Shall we not suggest it, Theo? She has nowhere else to go."

"By all means, my dear. She would be a pleasant companion for you."

"I might be useful to her. I am not likely to have anything else to occupy me this summer."

Theo knew very well what this meant. He said, rather diffidently, "You could not expect to go on managing Richard's house and family for ever. He was bound to marry again."

"He did not have to marry that creature."

Theo said no more.

So Harriet came to the Parsonage—she really had no choice—and Louisa, deprived of so many of her former activities, concentrated her restless energy on the organised improvement of her unlucky guest.

"It is high time you stopped moping," she told Harriet, the first evening. "Perhaps you consider there is some sort of merit in being jilted, that it entitles you to behave like an invalid?"

"No, ma'am," whispered Harriet, her mouth trembling a little.

"Then the sooner you learn to overcome your weakness, the better we shall all be pleased. I must say that I have been rather shocked by your want of self-control—the violence of your feelings—but I believe this has been largely due to your having too little else to think about. A well-chosen course of study, a set of regular duties to perform: these are the things that strengthen the resolution, Harriet—not mooning by the lake or reading silly novels."

Accordingly Harriet's day began with two hours' practice at the pianoforte before breakfast, which was followed by a spell in the nursery, teaching Master Henry Capel to read. Henry was six, a grave rather shy child, who adored his Mama and was over-anxious to please her, a heartbreaking ambition, for Louisa was a good mother, but very strict and not easily satisfied. Four-year-old Georgy was more resilient, he had a distinct look of his Uncle Verney. Harriet was fond of both the little boys, and enjoyed looking after them when Nurse was busy with their baby sister. She did not much enjoy the serious reading and the plain sewing she was required to do for her own moral improvement. The rest of her day was filled with various little employments in the house or round the parish: Louisa was determined that she would have no spare time to waste.

Harriet did not try to rebel against this regime; she was a guest, it was not for her to complain, and in any case all the fight had gone out of her. When she was with Louisa she was perpetually conscious of herself as that most contemptible of failures, a female who had been too unguarded in her affections. But still she defeated Louisa's main object all the same; she was still just as much in love with Verney, and she thought about him continually.

Her thoughts were a great deal more sensible than Louisa would have expected. She might have been silly in her own behaviour to Verney, but she was not silly about him; even in the midst of her romantic daydreams she had been able to observe some aspects of his character quite acutely, and she was convinced that for all his dash and polish, he was essentially a countryman who loved his home and was happiest in the places where he belonged. He had often talked to her about the land, about the habits of animals and birds, and also about many interesting books he had read, for he certainly wasn't a fool—but the London life he knew had no connection with any of these things, and if he had gone back there, as the family suspected, he might soon get into deep water. Her notion of the dangers of London was limited; she had constructed in her mind a garish, noisy gaming-hell, with dissolute young men tossing off bumpers of brandy and staking a fortune on a single throw, while improper females known as cyprians or demireps paraded around in damped muslin dresses with nothing underneath. She knew this picture was exaggerated and ridiculous, and that most young men came through their adventures unscathed, yet a shrewd instinct also told her that someone who was lonely and uprooted and bitter might easily come to grief.

How could Sir Richard have sent him away, she wondered for the hundredth time, one hot afternoon in the Parsonage garden as she cut the lavender which grew in a thick grey hedge along the side of the lawn. The sun was roasting on her shoulders, and the dry, silvery-mauve stalks made her fingers sore, as she worked on steadily, trying to imagine what Verney could have done or said to make his brother so angry. Something to do with Julia, of course. All the disagreeable things that had happened lately were Julia's fault.

There was a light footfall on the gravel, and a woman's voice spoke her name. She looked up, and there was Julia herself, two yards away, watching her. Slim and graceful, she looked as exquisite as ever, her skin glowing in the rose-coloured aura of a pretty silk parasol.

"Oh!" said Harriet uncomfortably, feeling that her uncharitable thoughts must be visible all over her face. "Did you—I expect you came to see Mrs. Theo? She's gone to the village."

"So they tell me. Richard is with the Rector, and I thought it was time I paid a duty-call on my sister-in-law. However, I can talk to you instead; we hardly ever seem to meet these days, Harriet."

Harriet did not answer. Surely there was no need to explain away the coldness that existed between the Parsonage and the Hall?

Julia looked around her. "What a flourishing garden this is; how well Louisa's lavender grows. I don't suppose it would dare to do anything else."

Harriet could not help smiling. Julia's lightly thrown-off comment was so very ridiculous. And she could not help being a little glad, after so much solemnity, to hear someone laughing at Louisa.

She said, rather hastily, "Would you like to sit under the lime tree, Lady Capel?"

"No, I should rather help you with the lavender." Julia put down her parasol, took a small pair of scissors out of her reticule, and began to sheer off the long stalks with a practised hand.

Harriet was slightly taken aback by this kind offer. They snipped for a while in silence before Julia spoke again.

"I suppose you have not heard—that is to say—there is still no news of Verney?"

Harriet stared across at the neat façade of the Parsonage, windowpanes glittering in the sun. "I should be the last person to receive any news of Verney," she said quietly. "I am surprised your ladyship has not considered that."

"Please forgive me—I did not mean to distress you." Julia herself was a good deal distressed. "I thought that as you were living here with Theo and Louisa, you were bound to hear the matter discussed. I thought, you see, that Verney would write to Theo. It was all on my account that he was sent away, and it makes me feel so guilty. Richard is so attached to him, I would do anything to heal the breach between them."

"Well, I'm afraid I can't tell you where he is now," said Harriet, her antagonism melting. "I wish I could."

After a slight pause Julia asked her whether she had made any new sketches.

"Not just lately. Mrs. Theo considers drawing is a waste of time. Though I can't see why," added Harriet thoughtfully, "for she is always telling me to persevere with my music, and I play so badly that I shall never give much pleasure to anybody."

"Oh, but that is precisely the reason," said Julia, opening her eyes very wide. "If I was in her charge (which God forbid) Louisa would lock up the instrument and send me out to make studies of ivy-covered ruins. And you know I draw atrociously. There's no virtue in doing what you enjoy. Louisa thinks people ought to do things they dislike for the good of their souls; she feels obliged to make herself useful by looking after all our souls for us. Poor woman, it must be a thankless occupation."

Harriet choked slightly, and Julia immediately recanted.

"I should never have said that! How very shocking—making you laugh at your hostess in the middle of her own lavender hedge. Now what's the matter?"

"It's the way you keep talking about her lavender hedge. Oh dear, I haven't laughed so much for weeks. Mrs. Theo never laughs."

"Yes, she does. She laughs with her teeth when she thinks she ought to, without understanding why."

The portrait of Louisa was instantly recognisable. Pretty and confident as she was, there was something missing. The climate she lived in was curiously joyless.

Again Julia retracted. "She is my sister-in-law, I ought not to be so disloyal. Richard would not like it. Let us talk of something else."

Harriet could think of nothing but Louisa laughing with her teeth. Resolutely forcing her mind away, she began to talk about her drawing. She thought she had progressed as far as she could; she did not feel she would ever improve. It was rather disheartening. Julia understood at once; she had been faced with the same intangible barriers in her struggle to become a really accomplished musician. This led to an animated discussion, and they both stopped cutting lavender.

What a dancing mind she has, thought Harriet fancifully. And she is such a pleasure to look at. Her eyes are as clear as crystal. . . . All resentment forgotten, she was under Julia's spell once more.

"If only I could paint better," she remarked. "That is half the trouble. I know a little about perspective and composition but I was never taught to use colour properly."

"You need some more lessons. From a first-rate master."

"There's no one of that sort round here."

"I've had a scheme in view for some time," said

88

Julia slowly. "You know that Chloe has a little talent for painting? I wouldn't think of comparing her with you, but she does show some promise and it is the only thing she does better than her sister. Dear Kitty is so good, she plays and sings so well, and embroiders and nets purses and speaks French —and I am afraid this has had a discouraging effect on Chloe. She pretends she doesn't care and won't apply herself. Miss Pringle says she seems determined to grow up perfectly ignorant. I thought that if we paid special attention to her drawing and painting it might help to make her more amenable."

"I'm sure you are right. It is so horrid always being a dunce. Poor Chloe, I do feel for her."

"So do I. And I know just the man I should like to teach her. His name is John Vincent and he is an artist working in Bath, mostly in oils of course, but he has a particular gift for watercolours. I hesitated to suggest his coming over here to give lessons to a little girl of fourteen—but if you were also to become his pupil it would be quite different. And Chloe would be delighted. She wouldn't feel that she had to compete against you, because you are a grown-up young lady and not her sister."

Harriet was overcome by the prospect of having lessons from a proper artist who painted pictures and sold them.

"Would he come all this way, just for me and Chloe?"

"I believe so. He isn't making his fortune very fast in Bath. We could arrange for him to stay here for a night or two every month."

"I wonder what Mrs. Theo will think."

In fact there was nothing Louisa could do. Julia's offer was a very practical one, and if Harriet's grandparents had been there they would certainly have allowed her to accept. Louisa had to content herself with saying, rather sourly, that all artists were known to be immoral, and she hoped the girls would be properly chaperoned.

Mr. Vincent was written to, everything was satisfactory, and at last a morning came when Harriet walked up to the Hall in a flutter of apprehension with her portfolio under her arm.

She had been imagining an open-air lesson beside the lake on a brilliant summer's day; unfortunately the weather had broken; it was grey and wet with a biting wind. The first lesson would have to take place indoors. Undaunted, Julia had found an ideal site on the second floor landing, immediately under the glazed cupola that flooded the grand staircase with light. A drugget had been put down to protect the carpet, and the head gardener had been told to send in a selection of plants from the greenhouse, to provide a subject. There were stools and easels, and the new paintboxes that Mr. Vincent had brought with him from Bath.

He was a large, laconic man, as swarthy as a gipsy. Harriet thought he had a hungry expression, but perhaps this was simply because she knew he was poor and needed commissions. He soon had Chloe making a still life drawing of a Wedgwood urn. Chloe was overawed and much less saucy than usual. Mr. Vincent began to examine Harriet's portfolio; first the pencil sketches, which he studied, unnervingly, without comment, and then the watercolours.

"What's this meant to be?"

"The lake at sunset."

"More like a dish of buttered eggs."

"Yes, I'm afraid it is," said Harriet humbly.

90

"I suppose you talk to your sitters like that," remarked Julia's `cool voice behind them. "I expect you tell them how fat and ugly they are, and then wonder why you can't make yourself acceptable to the dowagers—in Bath of all places!"

Vincent grinned. "Miss Piper isn't a Bath dowager. She has a good deal of natural talent, and enough sense to recognise her shortcomings. That's why she wants them corrected."

Treating the group of indoor plants as a miniature landscape, he spent the next hour showing Harriet how to achieve the varied shades and textures of green, overlaid and interlaced, dense yet translucent, which had always baffled her when she tried to paint trees.

It was a very decorous lesson, no one had the smallest inclination to flirt. They were chaperoned, of course, though not by Miss Pringle, as Harriet had expected. Julia stayed up on the top landing with them all the morning, taking the greatest interest in everything that was going on.

2

John Vincent stayed two days at Wardley, and into that space packed four enlightening lessons. The weather improved soon after he left. Harriet and Chloe naturally wanted to try out some of the things he had taught them, and not simply among the family scenes they knew by heart; with all the glories of the famous Wardley pleasure gardens to choose from, they were asking to go somewhere new.

Julia entered into their enthusiasm. "You want to paint something picturesque and a little out of the way; a blasted oak, for instance. Surely there must be several to choose from on the estate?"

"Not as far as I know," said Sir Richard.

"How very disappointing. What is the use of owning a quarter of Wiltshire, if you cannot produce a single blasted oak?"

"I'm going over to Spargrove tomorrow. There's a very fine midden in the farmyard there, would that be an acceptable substitute?"

"No one wants to paint a midden," objected Chloe, who had been taking this conversation quite seriously. "Oh, Papa—you are teasing us! How can you be so provoking?"

"It is a shocking thing to say," remarked Julia, "but I'm afraid your Papa has no sensibility."

"Now that is a deadly insult," said Sir Richard, smiling at his wife. "You will have to show me a good deal more respect, my love, if you want to join my exploring party to Spargrove."

Harriet thought that the glances these two exchanged were so full of love and laughter they were like shafts of dazzling light. The effect of their happiness was almost intoxicating.

It was agreed that they should all go to Spargrove, which was a property of Sir Richard's in an isolated hamlet some way from Wardley. They set off next morning under a cloudless August sky: Sir Richard driving his barouche, with Ned on the box beside him; Julia and Harriet, Kitty and Chloe surrounded by picnic baskets and paint boxes, and Dick (who was home from Eton for the holidays) riding down the leafy lanes ahead of them on his bay cob, and waiting at the corners for them to catch up.

Mr. Hawkins, the tenant of Spargrove, was a redoubtable yeoman farmer, a keen stock breeder and therefore a great ally of Sir Richard. Today, however, he looked less than delighted to see his landlord, perhaps wondering how his wife was going to entertain such a large party without any warning. Poor Mrs. Hawkins came running out of the farmhouse in her apron, to be quickly assured that they had not come to dinner; they had brought their picnic collation with them in the barouche. She accepted the picnic as a genteel whim, but still could not believe that Her Ladyship and the young ladies wanted to stay out in the hot sun; she kept offering them comfortable chairs in her front parlour. After a great many polite refusals they finally convinced her they were all mad, and she departed indoors, clicking her tongue. Sir Richard went off with Hawkins to inspect the farm, taking his two boys with him, and the artists were able to look around them for something to paint.

The farmhouse itself was too plain and square to arouse much interest, but there was a splendid old timbered barn, a ripe cornfield ready to be cut, and some mares and foals, charmingly grouped, in the shade of a chestnut tree that Gainsborough might have envied. Chloe decided at once that she wanted to draw the grazing mares.

Harriet turned away from the farm and walked a little way back up the lane, in search of something that had caught her attention as they drove by: the old manor house of Spargrove standing empty in a wilderness of passive desolation.

Spargrove Manor and all the land around had belonged to an absentee landlord, a prodigal who was always wanting money to pay his never-ending debts; Richard Capel had bought the land, acre by acre, and put in Hawkins as his tenant at the farm; last year he had bought the house, more from

93

generosity than anything else, for it was a decided encumbrance; the roof leaked, many of the windows were broken, and the carriage drive had disappeared under a tide of nettles. No one had lived there for twenty years.

Harriet skirted an ancient yew hedge that badly needed clipping. Presently she came to a gap through which there was a good view of the house. Studying that grey Elizabethan shell, she remembered how often she had tried to conjure up an atmosphere of archaic mystery in sketches of Lady Adela's Bower, the Nunnery, or even Bell Cottage. She had never entirely succeeded, and she now saw why. Those places were none of them really old or really deserted. Here was a house where people had lived for two and a half centuries, and which they had abandoned. It was not sinister or disagreeable, yet it was curiously haunted, as though the men and women of long ago were listening in the silence for the sounds of living to begin once more.

Julia had wandered up the lane behind her; she went through the gap and began prodding about for treasures in the choked flower beds of the neglected garden.

Harriet sat down on an old stone bench and worked out her composition. A rough, dark branch of yew would act as a frame in the foreground of her picture. Then, if she could get the perspective right, the eye must be led between the narrowing lines of the enclosed garden, right up to the house, which must be given an air of distance that was not merely physical, but in the poetic sense remote. Now that she was observing more carefully, she noticed that there was a trampled path through the rough grass and weeds—it was probably a short-cut between the fields and the farm. Would it be a good idea to put in a human figure? She pencilled a faint outline, looked up again, and nearly fell off her bench.

A figure had in fact appeared from another break in the hedge, and was walking along the grassy path, just where she would have placed him—the figure of a slim young man wearing a coarse linen smock and corduroy breeches. He was bareheaded, and the sunlight on his brown hair shone like polished copper. He moved with an impatient, springy stride she would have recognised anywhere.

"Verney!"

He stopped dead, stared at her in consternation and turned, as though he was going to bolt for cover. At that moment Julia appeared on the other side of him.

"Good God, Verney—what are you doing here?"

Trapped between the two of them, Verney seemed to have a confused impression that he was being hunted deliberately, for he said angrily to Julia:

"Who told you where to find me? Why can't you leave me alone?"

"No one told us—we hadn't the smallest expectation of finding you. We are here on a family expedition, nothing more. Richard had some business with Hawkins, so we decided that we must all explore to Spargrove."

"Oh, I see. I beg your pardon," he muttered awkwardly.

"But Verney, why are you here? You aren't—surely you cannot be living in that ruin?" She glanced towards the broken windows of the manorhouse.

"Among the rats? No, I've not yet fallen so low. I'm at the farm. I made Hawkins promise not to give me away when I came here three weeks ago from Holkham."

Holkham, thought Harriet: where Coke of Norfolk lived, the pioneer of improved farming. So that was where Verney had been. She did not attempt to join in the conversation, remaining seated on the bench and pretending to go on with her sketch, but she could hear every word that was said.

"So that's why the Hawkinses were so uncommonly put out by our arrival! But I still don't understand you, Verney," said Julia reproachfully. "Do you mean to tell me you have been within riding distance of Wardley for the past three weeks and never let Richard know? Why, he has been so anxious, he has been writing round everywhere, trying to get news of you. I hope you don't mean to go on quarrelling with him."

"The quarrel was not of my seeking. He threw me out of the house."

"Yes, and regretted it immediately afterwards. He is ready to acknowledge—that is, I am almost sure—I believe he would admit that he was in the wrong."

"Would he? Did he tell you why he was so angry, Lady Capel?"

Julia flushed a little, her face was partly hidden by the brim of her wide straw hat.

"You did not want him to marry me. But it is done now, and I hope you will be able to accept the *fait accompli* so that we can be friends. Friends enough, at any rate, to satisfy your brother."

Verney shifted undecidedly, as though he might plunge through the hedge at any moment and vanish.

"He doesn't know I'm here—"

"He is bound to find out. Hawkins may keep your secret, but that talking wife of his will let something slip, or one of the men. Imagine how painful that would be for Richard, to know that you refused to meet him. Besides, you can't keep it up for ever. Why don't you go to the farm straight away and get the whole business done with? If you meet again as a matter of course, and in the presence of strangers, I am sure you will find it a great deal less of an ordeal than you suppose."

Verney hesitated, then he made up his mind. He came on down the garden, passed Harriet at the opening in the hedge, and set off along the lane towards the farm as though he was facing a firing squad.

"Oh, I do hope Sir Richard will be kind to him!" exclaimed Harriet, as soon as he was out of earshot.

"I am persuaded that he will, if only from the relief of knowing that he is safe and well. We have been imagining him in all sorts of scrapes."

"Yes, so have I. And all the time he was at Holkham. It was stupid of me not to think of that, for I might have guessed he would rather be there than in London."

"Might you?" asked Julia, curiously. "Did Verney confide in you that he has a taste for agriculture?"

Harriet remembered what a fool she had made of herself by assuming that she understood all Verney's concerns. She pretended not to have heard Julia's question, and went on with her sketch, though she was now drawing so badly that she tore off the sheet of paper and screwed it up in disgust. The long, hot morning dragged interminably. Presently she rejoined Chloe in the field by the farm.

Chloe had made quite a pretty picture of the mares and foals, and Kitty had collected a great many berries and seedheads. Now they were thirsty and bored. Harriet sat beside them on the grass at the appointed picnic place, while Julia strolled up and down under the trees, apparently unable to settle. In due course the boys arrived, Dick full of the news that his Uncle Verney was staying at the farmouse; wasn't that the most extraordinary circumstance you ever heard? Still there was no sign of Richard or Verney.

Julia suggested that they should unpack the baskets of food, fetch a jug of water from the well. At last the two brothers were seen coming towards them along the edge of the cornfield. Richard was in front, his expression set and serious, and Verney lagged a few yards behind. However, they were obliged to walk single file, so it was impossible to tell what sort of terms they were on. Harriet glanced apprehensively at Julia.

Julia was equal to the occasion. "I am so glad you have brought Verney with you," she called out, as soon as they were close enough. "For the children are all wanting to see him."

This reminded both the men that they had got to be on their best behaviour, and gave Verney's nephews and nieces a chance to ask a lot of questions. By the time they had finished, everyone was sitting down and eating cold chicken.

They talked painstakingly about the marvels of Holkham, the splendid beasts, the rich fertility of that once-barren soil, and the strangely informal household, where guests were welcome to arrive uninvited and stay as long as they pleased, provided they fell in with the ways of their host, who at fifty-seven still put on a smock and went out with his men to work in the fields.

"And do you also intend to become a farmer?" Julia asked Verney.

"I hope to. If I can use my capital—"

"We shall have to see how you go on," said Richard, addressing him directly for the first time since the picnic began, but still not looking at him. "We think Verney had better remain here for the time being," he said to Julia, "and learn everything Hawkins can teach him, "but I have said he may come over to Wardley whenever he chooses—if that is agreeable to *you*, my love."

"To me? Why, certainly—you must come as often as Mr. Hawkins can spare you, Verney, and stay as long as you like. Your room will always be kept ready for you."

Julia's manner was almost gushing in her anxiety to make it clear that Verney could come home—for Richard had left the decision with her. He had practically said: this brother of mine has insulted you, and unless you are willing to receive him he can remain unforgiven.

"It is very kind of you," said Verney in a low voice.

The past was to be buried, but neither of the brothers felt at all easy in each other's company.

Harriet saw and heard everything, a solitary outsider among seven Capels. She was thankful for the violent family crosscurrents which prevented Verney from thinking about anything else. After that startled recognition in the garden, he had taken no further notice of her, perhaps he had forgotten, in the confusion of his feelings about his brother and Julia, that Harriet had made a public spectacle of herself on his account, and that people thought he had jilted her.

It was humiliating to feel oneself becoming invisible—but better than being singled out in everybody's mind for pity and contempt. Louisa had so preached at her about her past mistakes that she now had a positive horror of wearing her heart on her sleeve or attracting any kind of attention. It was enough to feel as she did on seeing Verney again —half sick with love and despair and a stupid trembling of excessive relief because he was safe—anonymous silence was the only tolerable disguise for such telltale emotions.

Once she was obliged to offer him a dish of plums. He took one, and said, "Thank you, Harriet," but he remained completely preoccupied.

Harriet shrank a little further into her shell.

3

"I see you are proposing to ride this morning," said Louisa, rather sourly observing the dark green habit which Harriet was wearing at breakfast about ten days after the expedition to Spargrove.

"If you don't require me for anything here."

"Are you meeting my nieces?" enquired the Rector.

"Yes, sir. And Lady Capel is coming too. She wants to call on Mrs. Daly, and in this weather it will be much quicker and cooler to ride through the woods, instead of trundling along a dusty road in the chaise."

"A ramshackle way to pay a call," commented Louisa. "However, I suppose she knows no better. . . . I hope you are not attaching yourself to this cavalcade, Harriet, because you think Verney will be there to open the gates for you. He went off to Spargrove again last night."

Harriet did not reply. She already knew that Verney had returned to Spargrove. He had been coming and going between the two places fairly frequently, and it was extraordinary how she seemed fated to be reminded of him, of where he was and what he was doing, even when she did not try to find out. She kept out of his way as much as she could. It was not that she disliked being in his company. She was no more unhappy seeing him than not seeing him. What she disliked was to be in company with Verney and Louisa at the same time, knowing that every word, every glance, was critically weighed up so that she could be reproved afterwards for having been too forward and effusive, or alternately too stiff, stupid and ungracious.

"At all events, I am sure you will have a pleasant ride," said the Rector, smiling at her apologetically.

Harriet sometimes wished he would stop his wife tormenting her; he often looked guilty and concerned, but never brought himself to the point. Although Louisa was consistently amiable to him, she was very short-tempered these days with everyone else in the house, and Harriet suspected that the Rector was only too thankful to have his wife's attention diverted from the servants and the children.

The groom brought Harriet's horse round to the door soon after half-past ten. The riders from the Hall had not yet arrived; Harriet mounted, and walked her horse down to the lodge gates. Looking out casually, she noted a curious group on the far side of the road—a shabby gig was drawn up on the grass verge with two people sitting in it: a thin, sallow man in a black suit, and a plump woman who appeared to be in some state of anxiety from the way she was plucking at the fingers

of her cotton gloves. She might have been a respec-
able shopkeeper or upper servant, the man was
more like a clerk. They had the air of townspeo-
ple completely incongruous in that Arcadian setting. Both were staring hard at the entrance to
Wardley Hall.

"Who are those people, Hooker?" Harriet asked
the old lodge keeper. "What are they doing there?"

"That's more than I can tell, Miss Harriet. They
were hereabouts most of yesterday, and when I
asks the fellow his business he says he's feasting
his eyes on this beautiful bit o' scenery. It's mighty
queer what gives some folks pleasure. If he thinks
the onions and carrots in my back garden are beautiful bits o' scenery, I can't hardly send him packing, just for being a dang fool!"

"You ought to be flattered," said Harriet, laughing.

She had heard the sound of approaching horses
and trotted off to meet Lady Capel and her step-
daughters.

Kitty and Chloe were in fine fettle. They had
learnt some passages from *The Taming of the Shrew*
and were going to perform them to amuse Mrs. Daly.
Maria Daly was waiting to be confined, and the
object of the visit was to raise her spirits.

"Chloe's Petrucchio would get anyone out of the
dumps," said Julia. She was wearing a pale blue
habit, frogged like a hussar's uniform, and riding
her favourite hack, a very pretty chestnut mare that
had been one of Sir Richard's many wedding presents to her.

"Papa laughed at us last night, didn't he?" said
Chloe. "And poor Pringle was in a fever because she
has a notion that some parts of the *Shrew* are quite

improper, only she is not sure which. She would rather we never read anything but *Julius Caesar*."

They had just reached the lodge gates, Chloe was in the lead with Harriet and Julia immediately behind her. It was difficult to say what happened next. Harriet heard Julia give a gasp of fright. She was clutching tightly at the reins, pulling on them so hard that the mare reared up, cavorting and slithering on the gravel. For a horrifying moment it seemed as if she was going over on her back; then she righted herself, agile as a cat, but Julia was pitched out of the saddle and lay quite still on the ground.

Harriet kicked her foot free from the stirrup and jumped down.

"Lady Capel—are you hurt?"

To her great relief, Julia raised her head and said, "How did they—where is she?"

"There's nothing to be afraid of, Sutton has the mare." Julia must have expected to be crushed by that fearful weight on top of her. "Do you think you could get up?"

Julia managed this quite easily. They were all crowding round: Sutton the groom, the two girls, the old lodge keeper. Kitty was a prey to acute sensibility, she was not able to be much help, but Chloe said (rather unnecessarily) that she knew how to set a broken limb, while the old man fetched a chair from his lodge and begged her ladyship to sit down on it.

"It's very kind of you, Hooker, but there is not the smallest need—I am perfectly well."

Julia stood staring around her and Harriet, following her gaze, made a mental note that the road outside was now empty; the couple in the gig had gone.

This hardly interested her; she was more concerned with taking care of Julia, who was extremely pale and clearly not fit to go on with the ride. They began to walk slowly up the drive, Julia leaning on Harriet's arm.

After a moment she whispered, as if to herself, "Oh God! What am I to do?"

Harriet was flurried and preoccupied, her intelligence was not at its keenest, and she took this at a very prosaic level, saying: "We can put off our visit to Mrs. Daly, you know. Tomorrow will do just as well."

"Oh—to be sure. Maria won't mind."

The Rector came hurrying to meet them, he had seen the whole episode from the parlour window. "My dear Julia, what a disagreeable fall, I do trust you aren't in great pain. You must come into the house and rest. I'll send round for the phaeton so that I can drive you home."

"I shall be very glad to get home, Theo, but I don't want to trouble Louisa—"

However he was insistent, shepherding them both up the steps into the Parsonage, where Louisa received her sister-in-law with a great deal of Christian charity banked up with coals of fire.

Julia was led into the drawing room and persuaded to recline on the sofa, hartshorn and a vinaigrette were produced, and the curtains drawn to keep out the sun. Louisa was considerate and capable, perhaps in some strange way she resented Julia less while she was in a position to look after her. Even if a hint of patronage inevitably crept in.

"What a pity you have stained the sleeve of your jacket. Of course these fashionable colours don't stand up to country wear. They never look quite the thing."

"It's of no consequence," said Julia, refusing the challenge. "I—what was that?"

The doorknocker banged and there was a sound of commotion in the hall. Julia jerked upright, her lips parted in terror. The fall had certainly had a shocking effect on her nerves.

Richard burst into the drawing room. "They said there was an accident—Julia?"

He saw his wife on the sofa and was beside her in an instant, leaning over her and grasping both her hands.

"My dearest love, my darling—thank God you are safe! That brute of a horse—I ought never to let you out of my sight."

"It was nothing, Richard. Merely a little tumble."

"That's all very fine," he said gently scolding her, her, "but you might have been killed, and as for me, I have died about a hundred deaths in the time it took me to run here from the stables."

Harriet wondered flippantly whether Louisa would offer him the vinaigrette.

He had by now noticed his relations; he asked Louisa whether they should send for the apothecary.

"Why, what could he do? Simply tell Julia that she will have a few bruises tomorrow—which I am sure she is perfectly resigned to," added Louisa, giving credit where credit was due.

"I suppose you are right." He switched to another subject. "What came over the mare? Sutton said she reared up for no reason. She's never done that before."

"It was my fault," said Julia. "She shied and I was startled; I must have pulled her head back too sharply on a short rein."

"What made her shy?"

"There were two people in a gig on the other side of the road," volunteered Harriet. "Perhaps they made some movement which frightened the mare."

"What people?" Julia's voice was suddenly shrill. "I didn't see anyone."

"Why, my love, you are trembling," said Richarl, who was still holding one of her hands. "I think you have been a good deal more shaken by this affair than you are willing to admit. You are as white as though you had seen a ghost."

"No, am I?" Julia tried to smile. "How very ridiculous."

4

The events surrounding Julia's accident left Harriet with a curious sensation of uneasiness, though she was not prepared to say why. The following morning, as in duty bound, she and Louisa went to make the proper enquiries. Julia assured them that she was completely restored. A little stiff, of course, but none the worse. She looked washed-out and haggard, fidgetting all the while she talked to them in her pretty dressing room, and starting at every footsteps that echoed up from the stone hall below. But perhaps she was merely suffering from the weather. It was uncomfortably hot.

Two afternoons later Harriet again saw the person she thought of as the man in the gig.

She was in the breakfast parlour at the Parsonage, writing a dull letter to her grandmother. Glancing out of the window she saw him crossing Church Green. Not in a gig this time, but he was unmistakably the same man, small and pale in his neat blacks; surely it was not fanciful to feel there was something ominous in his presence, as though he was a harbinger of doom. He reminded her of a raven.

She heard the knocker strike; then Hatton opening the door. A few words were exchanged, the door closed, and the visitor took himself off towards the lodge.

He must have some business with the Rector, Harriet told herself. She got up, all the same, and went in search of information.

Hatton had already vanished through the door that led to the servants' quarters, but Harriet was able to answer her own question. There was a table at the bottom of the stairs where any notes or cards that arrived at the house were displayed on a silver salver. Here she found a letter which had not been there ten minutes ago. It was addressed to Mrs. Theophilus Capel in a meticulous copperplate hand.

Louisa was out in the park with her little boys. Harriet knew that being inquisitive about other people's correspondence was an unforgiveable sign of ill-breeding. In spite of this, she was hanging around in a strategic position to greet her hostess when she returned half an hour later.

"Did you have a pleasant walk, ma'am?"

"Yes, we went to the lake to feed the swans . . . Henry, Georgy, run upstairs to Nurse. Smartly now! You know I do not like to tell you things twice."

Henry and Georgy trotted obediently upstairs. Their mother noticed the letter on the table, picked it up and carried it into the drawing room. Harriet followed her.

"Henry is learning to recognise a great many different trees and plants," remarked Louisa. She had put the letter down on a chair. Now she took it up again, reached for an ivory paper knife and slit the wafer without much interest, still talking about the child. "So many of the Capels have been botanists; I'm sure Sir Richard would be pleased if his nephew— Good God!"

She was reading now, grasping the single sheet of paper as though she was trying to tear every scrap of meaning out of it.

"I knew it," she exclaimed. "That wicked, abominable creature! I always knew what she was! Why didn't he listen when we tried to warn him?"

"What is it, Mrs. Theo? What's happened?"

Vulgar curiosity was rewarded. Louisa was so overcome that she passed the letter to Harriet without even considering whether it was suitable for an unmarried young lady.

Harriet raced through the contents.

"Honoured Madam,

"I feel it my duty to acquaint you with certain distressing facts regarding an individual who has recently become a member of your Distinguished Family. Three years ago Miss Julia Johnson was residing on the outskirts of Bath as nothing more nor less than a kept woman. In the spring of 1808 she was placed in lodgings at Widcombe Crescent by the gentleman who then enjoyed her favours. There can be no doubt as to the nature of this Guilty Association, for I am able to produce a signed statement of a Respectable Witness who found them together in Disgraceful Circumstances. I believe may wish to obtain possession of this Document (in order to prevent its falling into the Wrong Hands) and therefore beg leave to suggest that you or your Agent should apply to me at the Goat and Compasses Inn at Southbury, in order to Discuss Terms.

> "I remain, Dear Madam,
> Your humble Servant,
> A. Henchman."

"It's not possible," breathed Harriet. "A kept woman—disgraceful circumstances—I cannot believe that any of this refers to Lady Capel."

Louisa was believing it without the smallest difficulty.

"If only we had known this in time to stop the wedding. If Coverdale had done his work properly—"

"Coverdale?" repeated Harriet.

"The London attorney who has charge of all the Capel interests. I wrote to him when that creature first got her claws on Sir Richard, suggesting he should look into her antecedents—and got an impertinent reply, as good as telling me to mind my own business. Well, it is a pity Mr. Coverdale was too dilatory to mind his client's business; Sir Richard might have been spared a great deal of suffering. For I am afraid there is no doubt that he will suffer, when he discovers how cruelly he has been deceived. However, we must be thankful for small mercies; there need be no open scandal. People may guess what they choose but the true circumstances need never come to light. So long as we are rid of that jumped-up adventuress ladyshipping it about with her sensibility and her harp. . . . Now, what must I do? Theo's too scrupulous to deal with a matter of this kind; how lucky he chose today to visit his uncle. But Verney's at the Hall again. I can get him to make terms with this Henchman."

She was talking to herself, hardly aware of Harriet's presence. Breathing fast, under the pressure of emotion, her pink and white complexion unusually red, her china blue eyes standing out, bright and hard. Harriet watched and listened in growing dismay.

"Are you hoping that Sir Richard will disown his wife on the strength of this story?"

Louisa came to her senses with a jolt. "I ought not to have shown you that letter. I was so excessively shocked that I didn't know what I was doing. You must absolutely forget the contents; put it right out of your mind. When Sir Richard and Lady Capel —if there were to be a separation—I'm sure you know it would be most indelicate for a young girl to speculate on the reasons."

"Yes, ma'am," said Harriet automatically.

Surely Louisa must remember what it was like to be a young girl?

They dined in silence, both too preoccupied to make conversation. Harriet knew Verney had been summoned from the Hall; she did not require any hints to send her up to her room before he arrived.

She sat in the half light, her mind adrift in a sea of ambiguity, doubt and dread. Of course that horrible story could not be true, not literally so; there must be some explanation. (And there was quite a lot that needed explaining.) There was also the problem of Louisa; Harriet had realised for some time that the Rector's good, capable, sensible wife was a little unbalanced on the subject of her sister-in-law. If she exerted her influence on Verney (who had his own reasons for disliking his brother's marriage) the result might cause endless misery to the whole Capel family. There ought to be someone around to prevent this, but she could not imagine who.

Presently she came to a decision. Creeping quietly downstairs, careful not to disturb the conference in the drawing room, she slipped out of the house by a side door.

It was still very warm; the evening air lapped softly on her bare arms. She went through the lych-gate into the churchyard. There was a faint green radiance at the very top of the sky; in this subaqueous light the church stood out like a great cliff. Harriet was able to read the inscription on the nearest tombstone, extolling the virtues of one Martha Baxter. ". . . Sober, Dutiful, Diligent in Good Works . . ." What a dull life the poor woman must have led.

The clock in the tower chimed away one quarter after another. "Departed this Vale of Tears . . ." Harriet traced the lettering with her thumb; it was now too dark to read. With every minute that passed she became more nervous and despondent about her plan. She could guess what Verney would think when she intercepted him: that she was chasing him again, perhaps even trying to trap him. He would despise her, and she would shrivel up in anguish and despair. Much better creep home again, and let the Capels manage their own scandals. As she came to that conclusion, a thread of lamplight filtered across the steps of the Parsonage. Verney was leaving at last. He walked over the grass, a few yards from where she was standing. Harriet moistened her lips. This was the hardest thing she had ever had to do: calling his name.

"Verney!"

He stopped. "Who's that? Harriet? What are you doing out here at this time of night?"

"Verney, I must speak to you—"

"Not now," he said quickly. "It's much too late, and besides, you cannot expect me to meet you secretly in the churchyard! What do you take me for?"

"I'm sorry, Verney; I know it sounds dreadfully improper, but it's not because—nothing to do with —I mean, I have a special reason. I wanted to ask you what you mean to do about that letter?"

"What letter?"

"The horrible letter from A. Henchman. Are you going to show it to Sir Richard? That's what Mrs. Theo wants, isn't it?"

"Look here, Harriet, what the devil do you know about this?" he demanded. "How did you hear about the letter in the first place?"

"Mrs. Theo showed it to me."

"Then she shouldn't have done. I sometimes wonder if Louisa is taking leave of her senses."

"So do I. That's why I want to talk to you. I am sure Lady Capel is being falsely accused, only Mrs. Theo hates her so, she will try to make mischief with even the flimsiest evidence. I do hope you will consider what this may lead to."

"Wait a moment." Verney put one hand on the low wall, and vaulted over into the churchyard to join her. "Now, why are you convinced that the accusation is false?"

"I don't believe Lady Capel was ever a kept woman on the outskirts of Bath."

"Then where did this fellow Henchman get his information? Is he out of his senses too—a madman who goes round insulting the brides of baronets? I suppose that could be so. No one seems to have seen him."

It was a tempting theory, but it would not do.

"I've seen him," she said. "Twice."

"You have?" He listened grimly while she described the episode of the people in the gig.

"But my dear girl, surely you understand that this destroys your own case! Far from being a stray lunatic, Henchman is someone Julia undoubtedly recognised, and his presence in Wardley disturbed her so much that she fainted. . . ."

"She didn't faint. I think she tried to turn away so suddenly that the mare took fright, and that caused the accident."

"It comes to the same thing."

"Yes, I am afraid so," she admitted. "Lady Capel certainly knew the people in the gig; they must belong to a part of her life that she wants to keep hidden. I dare say she may have been imprudent —but that doesn't prove she was anything worse. She was very much alone in the world: I was wondering whether she came to rely too much—accepted more than she ought from some close friend, he might have been a man she expected to marry."

"You ought to be writing novels," said Verney, not unkindly. "Why are you so anxious to believe her innocent? Is it just because she is very beautiful and agreeable?"

"No, of course not. I'm not so green as that. But I'm sure she is also very good. She is so much in love with your brother."

"Let us say she is an accomplished actress."

"I call that monstrously unjust!" Harriet quite forgot to be humble in her determination to argue the point. "Why shouldn't she be in love? Surely you must know that your brother is handsome, gifted, a charming companion, a paragon of all the virtues women most admire. I am not at all surprised at Julia falling in love with him. There are much stupider men getting fallen in love with every day."

"Yes, to be sure," he agreed rather quickly, perhaps not wishing to discuss the point. "But what has this to say to anything Julia may have been doing in Bath three years ago?"

"I thought," said Harriet in a low voice, "that if a woman loved her husband so deeply—I thought such a woman could not have led a—a wicked life."

There was a short pause.

"My dear little Harri," he said uncertainly, "Surely you do not suppose that an immoral woman is incapable of being truly in love? You cannot be so simple."

Harriet blushed, thankful that it was too dark for him to see her face. She had been brought up to believe just that. Bad women were subject to violent and irregular passions which led to all kinds of disaster; only good women could inspire and experience that innocent gaiety, tenderness and affection which she had seen glowing so clearly through the whole family at the Hall. It now began to dawn on her that such an arbitrary division between good and evil was unlike anything else she had learnt to recognise in human nature.

"You think that Julia could have done those things and still make your brother so happy?"

"I see no reason why not."

"Then I don't see that it matters," retorted Harriet. "If a woman can commit an indiscretion and still be a good wife afterwards, I don't see why there is always so much fuss about girls being ruined."

"That is a very improper way of talking," pronounced Verney austerely. "You are too young to understand what you are saying."

She was rather pleased to find that this was the best answer he could manage; she had outflanked him with her sudden volte-face.

But it was an empty victory. In her heart of hearts she shared with Verney and Louisa a conviction so definite that it did not need to be stated; Sir Richard would never knowingly have married a woman who had once been another man's mistress. What would he do now, if he found out—or even suspected—that he had been cheated? Louisa thought he would send Julia away, and she was probably right. He had inflexibly high principles and he was not a man who forgave easily. Judging from his manner he had not really forgiven Verney for trying to stop him marrying Julia. She had done her best to heal the breach, she must know what he was like. No wonder she looked so wretched.

"Isn't it rather odd," said Harriet, "that Henchman has offered the incriminating statement to Louisa? Why didn't he take it to Julia? She's the person who stands to gain most by purchasing his silence."

"I think Henchman did go to her, but she hasn't got any money."

"Verney, she must have! My grandparents said that Sir Richard made her a very large settlement."

"So he did. The capital's all safe enough—in the Funds—only he doesn't seem to have made any arrangements yet for her to draw the income. I suppose he didn't think it important so long as they are down here in the country. There's nothing to buy in Wardley, precious little in Southbury, and when she orders anything from a warehouse, no doubt he foots the bill. She asked me yesterday whether she could borrow money from the Southbury Bank without his knowing. She laughed, and said, 'Pretend I am a hardened gamester, will they let me ruin my husband behind his back?' Of course I knew it was just talk—she hadn't any gam-

115

ing debts—I thought she was simply curious about the workings of a bank. But this evening, when Louisa gave me Henchman's letter, I saw what she was really after."

"And you told her yesterday that she wouldn't be able to borrow from the Southbury Bank?"

"Old Jones wouldn't lend her sixpence without informing Richard."

So it was impossible for Julia to pay Henchman whatever price he was asking—a stalemate which must have disconcerted him. He could have gone to Sir Richard—he must have threatened to do so. But whichever way Sir Richard took the attack on his wife's reputation, he would hardly hand out a reward to the person who made it. Far more profitable for Henchman to approach another member of the family; it was common gossip in the neighbourhood how much Louisa, in particular, disliked the marriage.

"Perhaps Mrs. Theo won't be able to raise the money either," said Harriet hopefully.

"That's already taken care of." Verney fished in his pocket and took out a pair of diamond shoe buckles, wrapped in silver paper. The settings were old-fashioned and absurdly ornate, but the stones were good.

"These belonged to Louisa's grandmother. She wants me to sell them."

"For blood money."

"That's nonsense. No one is going to be killed."

"I expect Julia will wish she was dead before you've all done with her."

Verney wrapped up the buckles. "I don't like this any more than you do. It's a dirty game, compounding with extortioners. And you may be right; there is a chance that Julia got into some scrape

116

which is being very much exaggerated. I'll have to know a good deal more about Henchman and his evidence before I decide what to do. I'll go into Southbury tomorrow and see what I can find out."

"Oh, I am so glad," she exclaimed, delighted by his reasonable attitude. "May I come with you?"

"On such an expedition? Certainly not. What a stupid question."

"I beg your pardon. I shouldn't have asked."

So vulnerable to his snubs, she couldn't keep the forlorn note out of her voice. He shifted uncomfortably.

"I didn't mean to hurt you, Harri. It's not that I don't want you with me, only you must see I cannot take you to places where you might meet a person like Henchman. You may drive with me to Southbury, if Louisa doesn't object, provided you keep away from the Goat and Compasses. Is that a fair offer?"

"Oh yes, thank you, Verney. I shan't be any trouble."

She knew why he had given in. He was conscious of having behaved badly to her in the spring, and he was afraid that his abrupt refusal had given her a false impression. It was humiliating, but she did not care. She was going to Southbury with him, to protect Julia if she could, and as for Louisa objecting, she wasn't going to have the opportunity. Harriet did not intend to tell her.

5

Harriet did not have to tell any lies. Louisa relieved her of the necessity by announcing at breakfast that she was going to visit Maria Daly, who was still waiting for the birth of her baby. She did not press Harriet to go with her, and Harriet guessed that she was regretting yesterday's confidences and wanted to avoid a tête-à-tête.

Verney and Harriet drove to Southbury. It was the first time she had been in his curricle since the cowslip-picking expedition which had raised so many false hopes. Today she sat beside him quite unaffectedly, too preoccupied to wonder whether people were envying and admiring her. She had got much thinner during the early summer, when she was eating very little and sleeping badly, and she had lost that bounding, childish exuberance which had done more than anything to make her seem such a large, amazonian girl. The new Harriet had a slender figure and a pleasing touch of reserve, as well as those speaking brown eyes which had always been her best feature.

They stabled the curricle and horses at the White Hart in the Market Square, and Verney said he would meet her there in an hour's time.

"I dare say you can amuse yourself by calling on one of your acquaintances."

"May I not walk as far as the Goat and Compasses with you? To make sure you find your man at home?"

"Oh, very well."

The inn which Henchman had given as his address was down a shady side street near the river. It was a small place but fairly genteel, not a low tavern.

Verney went in to make enquiries. If he did not return within three minutes she was under orders to go back to the centre of the town. As she gazed idly at the whitewashed front of the inn she saw a woman looking out of a downstairs window. She had a round, plain, anxious face, and Harriet knew her immediately. It was the woman who had been with Henchman in the gig.

They stared at each other for an instant; then the face vanished from the window. Harriet hesitated, uncertain what to do. At that moment Verney came out into the yard.

"Henchman's gone fishing," he said indignantly. "At least the tapster says he had words last night with Mrs. Sattle, and she's leaving on the Bath stage, so Henchman wants to keep out of the way until she's gone. What do you make of that? Who the devil is Mrs. Sattle?"

"She must be the woman who was with him in the gig, for I've just seen her looking out of that window. I took it for granted that she was Henchman's wife, but if she isn't— Verney, I've just thought of something! She must be the respectable witness. The one who made the signed statement. It was probably the sight of her that frightened Julia."

"Do keep your voice down, we don't want the whole town to hear. But I dare say you are right," he added gloomily. "I'd better tackle her instead."

He turned back into the inn, Harriet followed him. The tapster had now disappeared, and they found themselves in a narrow passage with several closed doors.

"She must be in there," said Harriet, pointing.

Verney tried the handle. The door opened into a frugal coffee room. Alone among the tables stood the gig-woman, wearing her best bonnet, with a small valise strapped and bulging at her feet. She had the flustered air of someone about to travel and not much used to it.

"Mrs. Sattle?" asked Verney genially. "I should be very glad to have a word with you, if it is convenient."

"I've nothing to say to you, young man! Nothing at all! Mr. Henchman assured me I need not answer any more questions. And besides, I have to go for my coach—"

"The Bath stage is not due in Southbury for another forty minutes. Won't you take a seat?"

"I have nothing to say to you," repeated Mrs. Sattle. She had a Somerset accent, overlaid by a thin refinement, and she was very uneasy. She kept on gabbling that she could not answer any more questions, while staring all the time at Harriet, who was still hovering in the doorway.

"Harri, you'd better go," said Verney over his shoulder.

Mrs. Sattle gulped. "Could I ask you, miss—I saw you that morning with Miss Julia—her ladyship, I should say—can you tell me, is she recovered from her fall?"

"Yes, perfectly recovered. Did you have a guilty conscience? I suppose you meant to frighten her?"

Mrs. Sattle burst into a flood of denials. She hadn't meant any harm, hadn't wanted to come, wouldn't have come either, only Mr. Henchman had said that if she wasn't careful they would send her to prison."

"What for?" asked Verney. Harriet had come right into the room and shut the door, but he was too preoccupied to notice.

"For contempt of court, sir. If I refused to give evidence. And if I did speak out in open court, I'd very likely lose my lease, for they would say I'd been keeping a disorderly house. Besides which, I couldn't bear the disgrace. I was very fond of Miss Julia, which is why I didn't do nothing at the time, but she had no right to impose on me. Deceiving me, like she's deceived that rich gentleman who married her. I'm a friendless widow, sir, with no one to fight my battles, and you can't blame me for not wanting to give evidence in a suit for divorce."

"Divorce!" repeated Verney in a voice of thunder.

Mrs. Sattle prepared to go into hysterics. Harriet produced a clean handkerchief and spoke to her in a rallying tone, feeling like a nursemaid with a large baby. While this was going on, she was dimly aware of a servant coming to the coffee room door, and of Verney giving him some money and saying they wanted the place to themselves.

Having had a chance to think clearly, he now asked Mrs. Sattle, "How long is it since you saw my—the lady we are speaking of?"

"The best part of three years. Until Mr. Henchman took me to watch outside that great mansion—"

"Then you have nothing to fear. If the lady's husband were ever to divorce her, he would not be allowed to call evidence about anything that happened before the marriage took place."

Mrs. Sattle gaped at him. "Are you sure, sir? Mr. Henchman said—"

"Mr. Henchman has tricked you for his own ends. You signed a statement and gave it into his keeping, I suppose?"

Mrs. Sattle nodded. It was doubtful if she understood exactly how Henchman had used her, but she was so angry, and at the same time so relieved, that she was quite ready to pour out everything Verney wanted to know.

She was the tenant of a house in the new Crescent at Widcombe, just above Bath. She let lodgings to gentlewomen. They were quite elderly, most of them, though sometimes there was a widowed mother with a daughter. She would not have been inclined to take Miss Johnson, a young lady quite on her own, but she was sorry for her.

121

"The poor thing had just lost her father, so her cousin told me, when he came and looked over the rooms. At least he claimed he was her cousin," said Mrs. Sattle darkly. "And how was I to know any better, with her in her blacks, and him visiting her regular to talk business—or so I believed at the time."

"Did he pay the rent?"

"Well, he did and he didn't. She'd give me the money, week by week, but he'd overlook the accounts, and it's my opinion that it was his money she was spending. She was with me the best part of a year, and they soon stopped pretending to be so formal in front of me, for I would go in with a tray or some such thing, and catch them holding hands—well, if they were sweet on each other, what was that to me? Of course I expected him to be out of the house at a decent hour of the evening," added Mrs. Sattle virtuously.

"Until one night my cat got shut indoors by mistake, and woke me, crying to be let out. I took him down to the kitchen, and on my way back I happened to glance into Miss Johnson's parlour and there was a gentleman's hat and coat, slung over the chair. Why, he's forgotten his coat, thought I —and just then I saw there was a light still burning in the bedroom, and I heard whispering and laughing. I—well, I won't disguise it from you, I did take one peep through the keyhole. After all, it was my house! And there they were on the bed —mother-naked—and the shameless things he was saying to her, I was never so shocked in my life."

Harriet was shocked too. In the literal, physical sense as though she had been kicked in the stomach. She had not supposed she could be so affected by the crude pictures that forced their way into her mind and had to be attached, with a shrinking imagination, to her idealised portrait of beautiful, elegant Julia.

Mrs. Sattle was babbling on. How she hadn't known what to do for the best, she ought to have turned miss out of the house, neck and crop, but she was too softhearted, that was her trouble. . . . In the end she had done nothing.

"What was the man's name?" asked Verney. His voice was cold as iron; Harriet could not bring herself to look at him.

"I never rightly knew," admitted the landlady. "She always spoke of 'my cousin.' That ought to have given me a hint, if I'd been sharper. Describe him for you, sir? Well, he was a long, dark fellow, not much above thirty, might have taken any girl's fancy. Quite a gentleman he was. Though there was nothing fashionable about him, he dressed ever so plainly, and always trudged up our hill on his two feet; I don't suppose he kept a horse. If you ask me, he couldn't afford to keep a mistress, for he never gave her any presents, except it might be a posy of flowers, or perhaps a book. I know they sometimes quarrelled about money. In the end he stopped coming, and I used to hear her sobbing her heart out, poor soul. Then she gave me her notice, packed up and went, without leaving a direction."

"And Henchman? Where does he come in?"

Henchman was an attorney's clerk who had arrived in Bath with some papers for Miss Johnson to sign, something to do with her father's estate. This was soon after Mrs. Sattle had discovered that Julia's lover was spending the night with her, and she most unwisely consulted Henchman and asked him what she ought to do. He advised her to turn a blind eye and raise the rent. Two weeks ago he had reappeared on her doorstep, told her that her former lodger was now the wife of an extremely wealthy baronet, who was anxious to divorce her.

"With all that stuff about how I'd been keeping a disorderly house, the nasty, shifty creature," said Mrs. Sattle wrathfully, "till I didn't know if I was on my head or my heels."

She could have continued on the subject of Henchman for some time, but just then the tapster looked in to say that Joe was ready to carry Mrs. Sattle's bag round to the Hart, and she had better go with him; the Bath stage was due there in ten minutes. She parted on the best of terms with Verney and Harriet. It was doubtful whether she knew —or would ever pause to wonder—whose side they were on. She was an amazingly stupid woman.

Verney left the room behind her. He soon returned, with a mug of ale for himself and a glass of milk for Harriet.

"I thought you'd sooner have milk; I don't trust their coffee." He placed the glass beside her. "I dare say you need sustaining."

She was grateful to him for not making any of the usual remarks about propriety and young ladies. He had sensed that by now they were in too deep.

"What shall you do?" she asked him.

"Get Mrs. Sattle's statement away from Henchman. That must be done, of course. But I'm damned if I want to be involved any further. Let Louisa do her own dirty work."

"I don't see how that will serve any useful purpose."

"I beg your pardon?" said Verney, sitting up very straight.

"Well, what will you accomplish by lurking in

the background? Your brother will be equally hurt by Mrs. Sattle's account, whoever brings it to his notice. You can't even hope to escape his resentment, for you know very well that Louisa will drag in your name and make out that your views are identical. Once you give her that paper, anything that follows will be your concern also, and I call it rather hypocritical to pretend otherwise. Though I do not wish to be uncivil," she added, as an afterthought.

"You are far too logical for a female," complained Verney. He hesitated for a moment. "I suppose you want me to destroy this wretched document?"

"Could you not do so?"

"I don't know. It's one thing simply to keep your mouth shut; quite another to tamper with the truth by suppressing a material fact."

It was the sort of distinction that men were always wasting time over. They had such complicated notions of honour. The only difference that mattered to Harriet was the difference between happiness and misery as it affected real people—the happiness or misery of Sir Richard and Julia, Kitty, Chloe, Dick and Ned. Why punish them all for the sake of something Julia had done three years ago, and perhaps bitterly regretted? She began an impassioned speech.

"You do not have to remind me," he interrupted her. "I know that Richard is likely to suffer as much as she does, I know how kind she is to those motherless children. Living as they are at the moment, she seems a perfect wife. But he intends to take her to London in the autumn, to reopen the Curzon Street house. They will entertain, move in a large circle of fashionable people. What has happened once may happen again. How long do you think she will be faithful to him?"

"For ever," said Harriet stoutly. "But then I disagree with your reading of her character. You have distrusted her almost from the start; I wonder why?"

"I felt that she was insincere, acting a part. Oh, not all the time. She is naturally good-humoured, has a talent for liking and being liked. It was her manner of receiving Richard's addresses that I could not stomach. So complaisant on the surface, yet so calculating and artificial."

"Artificial!" exclaimed Harriet. "We certainly don't agree about her. I have always admired her candour." The depth and spontaneity of Richard and Julia Capel's affection for each other had touched her particularly because her own family life was nothing but a polite sham. "Last time we dined at the Hall, when she was playing all your brother's favourite music on the harp, and when she was so taken up with his plans for the new cottages, so proud of his ability—did you think she was acting then?"

"No," said Verney slowly. "No, I must admit she has not given me that impression since I came home."

"Since they were married, in fact?"

"Yes."

There was a short pause.

"Perhaps you are right," said Harriet, "in supposing that she married for the sake of an establishment. Plenty of women have done that. But since she's now fallen in love with him, it doesn't matter any more."

"What a persistent little sea-lawyer you are, Harri. Nothing daunts you, does it?"

She was daunted by practically everything that

had to do with him. She did not know whether to be pleased or annoyed by this curious misconception.

He was busy allaying the last remnant of his own scruples. "That statement was obtained from Mrs. Sattle by a trick. If she had any say in the matter it will never be used."

"Then you do mean to destroy it? How will you pacify Louisa?"

"I am not precisely certain yet," said Verney evasively. "I'll think of something."

6

The notes of the harp quivered slowly through the air, like bubbles rising to the surface of a stream. Julia sat beside her instrument in that classic pose which always made a woman look so remote. Only her white arms moved against the golden frame; the beautiful profile and the graceful body were quite still, as though she was listening to her own music, those soft, melancholy Irish airs she played so well. This was another aspect of the lively, sparkling Julia who kept the household spinning round her so contentedly, but it was one that Richard found equally enchanting. She's bewitched him, thought Verney, watching his brother with a mixture of irritation and compassion.

She had deceived him once, when she married him; the question remained, was she likely to deceive him again? Harriet thought not. She thought that Julia's Bath liaison had been a solitary fall from grace, and that she must have suffered agonies of remorse before deciding to marry Richard. Verney had never seen anything in Julia that could possibly have been taken for remorse but he found himself admiring Harriet's loyalty, her generosity, and that quality of innocence which had nothing to do with ignorance; she was certainly not missish or squeamish. She was honest, delightfully different from schemers like Julia or Pamela Sutcliffe. It struck him that she had become a great deal less childish and more sensible in the last few weeks, and also that she was becoming very pretty, if you liked tall girls. Which he did.

The music splashed into a lively march, and Verney, studying his sister-in-law, marvelled at her composure. It was now four days since Henchman had first been seen in the district, and during that time she must have lived in constant dread of his betraying her secret to Richard. He had not done so, and perhaps she was beginning to believe that she was safe; she would hardly expect him to go to Louisa.

Louisa. She was at the centre of the dilemma. Verney was certain of one thing: if she was ever allowed to read Mrs. Sattle's story, nothing on earth would prevent her taking it to Richard. He would have to get hold of the written statement, destroy it, and then tell Louisa that the whole thing was a mare's nest, an impudent fraud. Meanwhile returning the diamond shoe buckles as a proof of good faith. She would be disappointed, but she would believe him. Blinded by her obsession, she took it for granted that he too was determined to ruin Julia and break up the marriage.

There was one serious obstacle to this plan. He was as helpless as Julia; without the diamond shoe buckles he had no means of raising the sort of money an extortioner was bound to ask for. His small capital was in trust, he had spent most of this year's income and nobody in the neighbourhood was at all likely to lend him several hundred pounds. He might consult Theo, who had never been hostile to Julia. But then Theo might think it was his Christian duty to pass on everything he was told to Richard. You never could tell with clergy, thought Verney gloomily.

Of course there were still the shoe buckles. Suppose he didn't hand them back? Suppose he sold them to pay Henchman and then told Louisa that they had been lost? He decided, regretfully, that this course of action would be not only dishonest but dangerous. She might not guess the connection between the missing buckles and the missing statement, but she would probably think he had sold the diamonds to pay a gaming debt. It was the sort of thing Louisa would think. She would complain to Theo, and perhaps to Richard as well, and there would be the devil of a family scene, during which the real facts would almost certainly come out. No, he couldn't touch the shoe buckles.

A procession now entered the music room; Smethurst the butler and two footmen with all the paraphernalia of the tea tray. The table was laid, the silver candelabra set in place, and they gravely withdrew. Julia stopped playing and came over to the table.

"That was charming," said Richard. "There is something magical to me about the harp. I could go on listening for ever."

"I never had a better audience than you and Verney."

"We have never been so well entertained. Which

129

reminds me, I collect that the girls are rehearsing some more scenes from Shakespeare?"

"Yes, and they have even persuaded Dick to take part."

"What's the play this time?"

Julia put down the cream jug. "They are learning some passages from *Othello*."

"Good God!" exclaimed Verney. He couldn't help it.

Julia was just handing him his teacup. She shot him a glance that was at once startled and speculating.

"*Othello!*" repeated Richard. "What an extraordinary choice. I don't know what Miss Pringle can be thinking of."

"It isn't Miss Pringle's fault, Richard. They asked me if they might do it, and I said yes. It never occurred to me that you would not like it."

"My dear Julia, you must have read *Othello*, even if you never saw it performed on the stage. It is full of lines that are totally unfit for Kitty or Chloe to recite, in fact the whole tendency of the play is altogether too dark and violent for the schoolroom."

Richard was always rather intimidating when he was annoyed. He put down his teacup and sat frowning, one hand on the arm of his chair. His white fingers, closing round the narrow spar of mahogany, reminded Verney, suddenly and irresistibly, of Othello's brown fingers pressing the white throat of Desdemona.

"I am very sorry that you are displeased," said Julia, mortified.

"I cannot imagine why they fixed on *Othello*."

"Oh, I can tell you that. The girls had set their hearts on a tragedy but Dick wanted a comic part.

He agreed to give way on condition that he was allowed to black his face."

Richard stared at her for a moment, and then burst out laughing.

"Of all the absurd reasons—I wonder what Kemble would say! My dearest girl, forgive me for behaving like a bear; I can see that it doesn't matter what those children do, it will be a farce from beginning to end."

She laughed with him, but Verney thought that she was not far from tears.

Later that night he wrote two letters, to be delivered by his groom early in the morning. The first was to Henchman at the Goat and Compasses. The second read:

"My dear Harriet,

"Since I have not the means to buy H. off, I am resolved to frighten him off. I have written to him, bidding him meet me at the west gate of the park (the one that has no lodge) tomorrow at three. I shall await him there with the barouche. When he arrives, I shall surprise and overpower him, and get possession of the written statement. After which I had intended to let him go, but on second thoughts I fear he might make trouble by running straight to L. So I have decided to tie him up and drive him to some remote place, perhaps on to the Plain, where I shall abandon him, having first removed his money. I may take his boots as well. After this treatment, I doubt if he will dare return to Wardley. It is a rough scheme, but the best I can devise. I am telling you this because I am very sensible how far your good

131

counsel has helped me to make up my mind.
I will come to see you when it is over.
Yours, etc.
V. CAPEL.
Burn this."

7

Harriet read Verney's note sitting up in bed, where
it had been brought to her by a giggling under-
housemaid who thought M. Verney must be sweet
on her.

At first sight the great scheme was a little disappointing; she would have liked something neater
and more subtle. Verney's solution was a hit-or-miss
affair, with no subtlety about it. But it would probably work. She agreed with him that destroying
Mrs. Sattle's statement would not be a sufficient
safeguard. Any risk of a meeting between Henchman
and Louisa must be prevented at all costs.

The last three lines of the letter gave her infinite
pleasure and astonishment. Far from Burning This,
she put it away in the drawer where she kept her
handkerchiefs, and returned to it several times during the day. At the fourth rereading she suddenly
perceived a weak link in Verney's arrangements.
How was he going to dispose of Henchman's gig?

He himself was going to the meeting-place in the
barouche. (It had to be a fair-sized carriage, you
could not conceal a bound man in a curricle.) Ob-
viously he could not take his groom with him to attend to the horses, and it was to be hoped that
they would stand still while he was assaulting the
extortioner; the whole performance ought to be over
in a matter of minutes. But there was a complica-

tion that Verney had apparently overlooked: What was to become of Henchman's gig after he had spirited away the owner? If he simply left it where it was, inside the west gate, this would draw attention to Henchman's disappearance, and curiosity would be centred on Wardley Hall. It would be much better if he could take the whole conveyance into the village: let the horse loose in a field, perhaps, and hide the gig in somebody's barn. But to do this he would be obliged to leave his own team standing alone for quite a long time, and with Henchman in the barouche, a prisoner under a rug. It would be a fearful risk. What Verney needed was an accomplice.

She knew very well that she was not the sort of accomplice he would have chosen, but it was too late to worry about that, already after half-past two. She had a pair of hands to hold horses with, and she was in any case the only person he could trust.

There was no one around to intercept her, as she hurried from the house, tying the strings of her bonnet. Directly she was out of sight of the Parsonage windows she began to run. Up the drive, down a grassy slope towards the Rustic Bridge, across to the other side, left-handed past Lady Adela's Bower, and then a long stretch to the far end of the lake.

There was going to be a storm, the weight and pressure of the sultry air was intolerable, and already a few isolated drops had fallen, as though the sky was sweating. Harriet pounded along in her blue gingham dress, her eyes fixed on the Cascade as it came splashing down over that highly unlikely group of Gothic rocks. Presently she was able to make out a dark blob which was the window of the submerged Grotto, less than a foot above the

133

surface of the lake. The wall of the park was a little way behind the Cascade, and the west gate not more than twenty yards from the Grotto. As she ran through the last clump of trees she saw the barouche. Verney had taken his horses right up to the gate and tethered the leaders to one of the iron rails. He was standing in the drive, watch in hand.

"Harriet! What are you doing here? Is anything wrong?" He came anxiously towards her.

She shook her head, too puffed to explain. "I thought—you'll need help—Henchman's gig," she managed at last.

When Verney finally understood why she had come, he was extremely annoyed.

"Certainly I considered the gig, I'm not a complete numbskull. I wrote that he was to stable his horse in the village and come here on foot."

"You didn't tell me that—"

"I'll tell you something now, my girl. If you keep trying to manage everyone's affairs, you'll end up just like Louisa."

"I'm sorry, Verney," she said, quite crushed by this frightful prediction.

"Well, you'd better go home before it starts raining. . . . No, wait." He lowered his voice. "I can hear someone on the road. I don't want Henchman to see you. Go into the Grotto, Harri, and stay there till I call you. And for heaven's sake don't try to do anything clever."

Harriet retreated obediently down the little flight of steps that led into the Grotto. Standing in the shell-lined outer chamber, she strained her ears to catch what was going on. The click of the wicket, a cautious challenge, words and movements—nothing was clear except that the two speakers were having an argument.

She stole silently back to the bottom step; she could now hear Verney quite distinctly.

". . . I am not paying a penny for any document until I have examined it personally."

"Come, sir—that's unreasonable. After all the trouble and expense I've been put to, I am entitled to some remuneration."

The voice was disagreeable, being both common and aggressive, with an unctuous imitation of gentility. Flattening herself into the shadows and staring upwards, she got a foreshortened view of the extortioner. He was older than she remembered and spiderishly thin.

"We'll see about that," said Verney, suddenly producing a pistol. "You can hand over that precious statement straight away, if you don't want to be shot!"

"You won't frighten me with that sort of talk!" jeered Henchman. "That toy ain't loaded—you wouldn't dare—" He lunged forward, and Harriet put her hand over her mouth to stop herself screaming.

Henchman was right; the pistol wasn't loaded. But it was a serviceable weapon, all the same. Verney caught him a crack with the butt on the side of the head, and he crumpled and collapsed on to the grass, where he lay insensible.

It was at this moment that Harriet caught the sound of voices somewhere behind her.

She darted back into the Grotto to the small window that was cut in the outer wall of the rock. Through this artificial crevice, a little above the level of the water, she was able to see the section of the bank immediately on her right, where the lakeside path began a short detour to climb the steep knoll behind the cascade. There were two ladies and two gentlemen walking along this path, chatting in clear, confident voices and glancing about them with the complacency of well-bred persons who knew they were enjoying the beauties of nature. They were moving quite fast, in spite of their raptures; directly they turned the corner and crossed the footbridge above the waterfall they would have an uninterrupted view of everything between the gateway and the Grotto—which at present included Verney, the barouche, and the unconscious Henchman.

She scrambled up the steps, two at a time. Verney was kneeling beside his victim, searching his pockets, a coil of stout cord lay on the ground beside him.

"There are some people coming—that tedious man Slingsby and some strangers. What are we to do?"

Verney straightened up. He looked at the barouche, measuring the distance with his eye.

"Have I time to get him stowed away?"

"No, you are bound to be seen. Shall we say he's fainted?"

"He may come round at any moment. I'll hide him in the Grotto until the coast's clear." He got to his feet, picking up the bundle of cord and the senseless body of the extortioner, who looked unexpectedly fragile and no longer in the least sinister. As he humped his burden down into the Grotto, he said, "You'll have to keep them out of here as best you can, Harri, there's a good girl."

Not a word now about unwanted interference. He was relying on her not to make a fool of herself.

She took up her post, gazing at the lake with a soulful enthusiasm she was very far from feeling. Her mind was blundering about like a mole in a trap. How was she to keep the visitors out of the Grotto? Mr. Slingsby, an impenetrably dull neighbour, was always bringing people over to admire the glories of the pleasure gardens, and the Grotto was his favourite haunt. She could hear him delivering a lecture as his party came over the footbridge.

". . . You will be particularly pleased, my dear Helen, with the figure of a Sleeping Siren that the sixth baronet brought back from Florence; there is a most romantic story of his obtaining this statue from the Palace of some prince or other—"

"There's somebody down there," broke in one of his companions. "A girl in a blue dress."

"So there is! One of the Miss Capels, I dare say. They are not out yet, but Miss Kitty is quite—No, it's Miss Harriet Piper!" He hastened over the grass to greet her. "My dear Miss Piper. How do you do? I mistook you for Miss Kitty Capel. . . . Helen, I am happy to make you acquainted with Miss Harriet Piper who lives at the Dower House with her grandfather, General St. John Boyce . . . My cousins Mr. and Mrs. Cutler and their friend Miss Nixon."

Mrs. Cutler, a proud sort of lady, looked disapprovingly at Harriet's crumpled gingham, but condescended to shake hands with her because she was the granddaughter of a General. Mr. Slingsby explained that they were walking round the lake (which was perfectly obvious) and that they had sent their carriage to wait for them at the Hall, as they intended to call on Lady Capel.

"If we are going to inspect this famous Grotto," said Mr. Cutler, "we had better do so as quickly as we can. The weather is not going to hold up much longer."

He started down the steps, and Harriet burst out in desperation, "I'm afraid it is not possible for you to see the Grotto today, sir."

"Not possible!" he repeated. "Why not, pray?"

"There is a crack in the wall of the outer chamber," she said, suddenly inspired. "We are afraid to let anyone go in, because of the danger of falling rocks."

At this juncture there was a sharp thud inside the Grotto, followed by the sound of a man swearing.

Miss Nixon gave a small scream, and Mrs. Cutler exclaimed: "There's someone down there already!"

"That's Mr. Verney Capel; he's gone to see how bad the damage is. I expect he'll be out again directly."

Harriet had raised her voice and moved a little nearer the entrance as she said this, and apparently Verney heard her, for he answered his cue and emerged from the depths, rather hot and flushed, which was appropriate, and talking gravely about having the cracks repaired before they got any worse. He winked surreptitiously at Harriet.

Mr. Slingsby was deeply disappointed. His cousins were annoyed with him, and showed it.

"So you've made us walk all this way on a wild goose chase," remarked Mrs. Cutler. "And we are going to get soaking wet into the bargain. I knew we ought to have stayed in the carriage. Now I suppose we are to walk another mile in the rain." And she looked rather pointedly at the barouche.

"I don't think I can go much further," said Miss Nixon in a die-away voice. "It is quite enough underfoot and my shoes are too thin."

Harriet sized her up as one of those women who

only went on expeditions in order to have a headache or twist her ankle. The rain was coming down really hard, and by now everyone was looking at the barouche.

"You must allow me to drive you to the house," said Verney. He really had no choice.

The visitors accepted thankfully without even pretending to hesitate. There was plenty of room for everyone, but Harriet hung back, uncertain what Verney would want her to do.

"Get in, Harriet, if you please," he said quite firmly.

He was not leaving her to guard Henchman, and in fact it was difficult to see what use that would have been.

Verney took them along the west drive at a rattling pace. The sky was now as dark as lead, the waters of the lake reflected a sullen glare, and in this metallic setting the grass and trees had turned a lurid, sickly green, such as you might expect to see in the swamps of a tropical jungle.

Since the hood of the barouche was closed, Harriet caught only fragmentary glimpses of this strange world. She was wondering what would happen if Mr. Slingsby started asking Sir Richard about the damage in the Grotto. It was the sort of thing he would do, she decided gloomily.

Verney drew up with a flourish at the front door, and they were told that her Ladyship was at home, but Sir Richard had gone to Southbury and was not expected much before dinner. This was a relief, even though it meant that Verney felt obliged to remain with the guests and act as a substitute host.

She glanced at him as they followed the footman into the house. She wanted to ask, what will hap-

pen to Henchman? Will he be able to get away?
Verney made her a pantomime face which told her
nothing.

Julia was in the small drawing room (so called
to distinguish it from the white drawing room and
the Chinese drawing room). She had Kitty and Dick
with her, and they were occupying a wet afternoon
by sorting the family collection of Roman coins.
This was the first time Harriet had seen Julia since
hearing Mrs. Sattle's uncomfortably vivid account of
what she had been doing three years ago in Widcombe. The joys and sorrows of that secret life—
those violent surrenders to passion and grief—it was
impossible to asociate them with the elegant Lady
Capel, secure in her husband's house and the company of her stepchildren. Did this make her seem
less guilty or merely more brazen? Unaware of
Harriet's scrutiny, she was saying everything that
was proper, and bearing with fortitude the tire-
someness of being called on by Mr. Slingsby.

The conversation was extremely dull, being entirely concerned with the storm that was tearing down
the valley in sheets of horizontal rain. Every few
seconds the sky was bathed in lightning. Each flash
of merciless brilliance was followed by its drumroll
of thunder.

Various people said that the effects were very
striking, that the weather would be much pleasanter now, and that the farmers needed rain.

"But hardly in this quantity," said Verney scornfully.

"We may feel better afterwards," faltered Miss
Nixon, "but I own I feel far from well at present.
Thunder does not suit my constitution. I know
you think me foolish, Helen."

"Well, I don't think you foolish, Miss Nixon," said Julia kindly, as it was clear that Mrs. Cutler was going to say something disagreeable. "Won't you change your chair, so that you can sit with your back to the window."

Under cover of the talk and movement, Verney managed to whisper to Harriet: "Don't look so worried. He's safely tied up and he can't escape."

Before she had time to answer they were almost blinded by a meteoric white flare. There was an instantaneous roar and then the noise of something heavy falling, immediately overhead.

Everyone jumped visibly, and poor Miss Nixon cast herself face downwards among the cushions, stuffing her fingers in her ears.

"We've been struck!" said Dick. "What a lark!" He ran towards the door that led into the hall.

"Don't go out there, you silly noodle!" Verney grabbed his nephew by the elbow, and they stood poised, listening to the high brittle octave of sound that rasped and shivered alarmingly above the wailing of the wind.

"What was that?"

"I think the weather vane must have come down on the central cupola. That was the glass from the cupola falling inwards on to the grand staircase."

Verney opened the door, and they could see a mass of broken glass trailed across the stairs in jagged spars like icicles.

"The nursery!" exclaimed Julia. "Poor little Ned, up there on the top floor, I must go to him at once—if you will forgive me, ma'am. My youngest stepson is only eight years old—"

"Don't mind us, Lady Capel. The storm is abating, and if our carriage may be sent for, we will take

141

our leave as soon as Matilda Nixon has come to her senses." Mrs. Cutler drew on her gloves, with a contemptuous glance at her afflicted friend, who was sniffing dolefully at her vinaigrette.

"Yes, indeed," said Mr. Slingsby fussily. "We must not put you out any further—outstay our welcome."

Verney had already ventured out into the hall; he said that he and Julia had better go up to the nursery by way of the backstairs. The butler appeared, looking solemn.

"Excuse me, Mr. Verney. What do you suppose Sir Richard would wish me to do about the pictures?"

"What pictures, Smethurst?"

"The paintings up there on the walls of the staircase, sir. The rain is blowing through the gap in the cupola, and they are all becoming extremely damp. In particular the Van Dyck," said Smethurst, who had the experienced butler's gift for imparting bad news with a mixture of detachment and oracular pessimism.

"Oh lord," said Verney, peering upwards. "Yes, you're right; they are getting wet. We can't leave them there. If you and the footmen will get some ladders and start taking them down, I'll join you as soon as I've escorted her ladyship to see Master Ned. We shall need some towels and—Harriet, would you superintend the drying and stacking of the pictures? We must take care that they don't get scratched."

"Yes, of course I will." She was glad to make herself useful.

There was so much to be done; neither Harriet nor Verney had time to think about the prisoner in the Grotto.

It was nearly six when Sir Richard came home. He had been soaked through earlier in the afternoon, and was now half dry, cold and uncomfortable. He stared bleakly round him and enquired: "What the devil's happened here?"

"Can't you see, my dear fellow? The duns are in," said Verney flippantly.

In fact the Capels' ancestral hall did look remarkably like the setting for an episode of *The Rake's Progress*. The furniture and paintings were all crammed in one corner (out of reach of the rain, in case it started again). The leaking roof, the denuded walls, with their dismal streaks of dust and unevenly faded patches where the pictures had been—taken all together, the impression was one of spendthrift misery with a moral attached.

Richard was too tired to be amused. "Don't be a damned fool," he snapped.

"Very well, if my efforts aren't going to be appreciated, I shall take Harriet back to the Parsonage. You don't mind walking, do you? The rain has quite stopped."

He gave her hand a slight warning pinch. Harriet knew they were not going straight to the Parsonage. She said she would be perfectly happy to walk.

Richard was now talking to Smethurst and made no attempt to stop them.

As they went out, Harriet said, "I am sure your brother did not mean to be cross. As soon as he learns from Lady Capel and Smethurst how much you have done to save the pictures, he will be very grateful to you."

"Yes, I know. That's why I wanted to escape before he found out. The whole business has lasted such an age, and I don't know what I'm to do about Henchman; it will look confoundedly odd if I take a carriage out at this hour. I can't pretend I'm going out to dinner, dressed as I am, and without a groom—good God!"

They had been hurrying across the wide sweep of lawn on the west of the house. Having reached the place where the ground began to slope away, they expected to see the lake lying below them in the beautiful and familiar shape of an hourglass.

But the hourglass had vanished. A formless expanse of water was lapping the sides of the valley, sweeping over paths and bushes washing around the trunks of trees. Lady Adela's Bower had a slightly Venetian air—only the gonola was missing —and the Rustic Bridge had become an absurd frivolity, a bridge that went nowhere, for it was entirely surrounded by water.

"Surely there wasn't enough rain—"

"No, but I expect the Lupton brook has got blocked again. It often does, you know, after a storm."

The lake was filled by a constant stream of running water that poured down the Cascade and was carried away at the opposite end by the Lupton brook, a sluggish rivulet which sometimes got choked. Whenever the water came in faster than it could get out, there was bound to be a flood.

A disturbing idea struck them both at the same instant. The far end of the lake was half-hidden among the trees. Together they ran forward to another vantage point and stood still, staring. There was far more water than usual rushing into the lake, not just in one slender scimitar of white foam; it was bubbling and seething all over the rocks which loomed above the Grotto. The rocks themselves seemed curiously dumpy, because the water level had risen over two feet. The flight of steps that Harriet had guarded that afternoon now plunged into a lagoon, and the crevice window had completely disappeared below the surface of the lake. The Grotto must be full of water, right up to the ceiling.

"Oh no," whispered Harriet.

Verney said nothing. He simply stood there, growing very white.

After a moment she said: "He may not be there. He may have got away."

"Not much hope of that. I tied his knees and ankles together, so that he couldn't walk, and then I took the same cord and bound his elbows to his sides and his hands behind his back, to prevent him undoing the knots. And I gagged him, to stop him calling out. How could he have got away? He's lying there in the inner chamber where I left him. Drowned. And it's my fault."

"No, it isn't, Verney. You weren't to know how things would turn out—"

"I should have remembered that the water was sure to rise in this weather. Poor devil, it doesn't bear thinking of. He was the meanest kind of criminal, a vulture who fed off the misfortunes of others —even so, I wouldn't have wished such a death on my worst enemy."

"Perhaps he never regained consciousness," she said, not very hopefully.

145

"He was nearly round when we left him. That's why I used a gag."

So Henchman would have known that he was going to drown. Lying there helpless in the cold and darkening Grotto, he could have heard the water flowing in, seen it spreading across the floor towards him, felt it reach his back, his chest, his throat. Straining at the cords, and not even able to scream . . . Harriet felt sick.

Verney slipped a hand through her arm, though whether to give comfort or receive it she was not certain, for she found he was trembling as much as she was.

"I never killed a man before," he said with a note of apology. "It's lucky I left the Army; I wouldn't have been much use on a battlefield."

She felt extremely sorry for him as they stood side by side staring at the sheet of water that had suddenly become hateful to them. The leaden tinge had gone from the sky, which was now a bruised purplish grey; the air of calm after the storm struck her rather as an air of desolation. She wanted to tell him that no one would blame him for Henchman's death, but decided that this insipid remark would be merely an irritation. Nor would it be in very good taste to point out that at least Julia's troubles were over. Besides, it might not even be true. She was aware of another frightening possibility.

"You never told me whether you got hold of Mrs. Sattle's statement?"

"There wasn't time," he said wretchedly. "I was just about to search him when Slingsby arrived, and once I got him into the Grotto I was in too much of a hurry getting him tied up. God, what a damnable bungle I've made of everything."

"Surely the paper will have been soaked into a pulp, do you not think so?"

"Yes, if we're lucky, but we dare not count on it. I can't help feeling that Henchman would have stowed it away in a leather purse or card case—after all, it was worth good money, or so he thought. I shall have to try to get it off the body, and remove the rope and the gag if I can."

"I don't see how you are to do that."

"By going into the Grotto as soon as the water has drained away sufficiently, and before anyone else does. After dark, if possible, to be sure I'm not seen. Not tonight, that would be too soon, but somewhere around midnight tomorrow the water should have sunk far enough. I'll have to chance it."

She was horrified and said so. Henchman's death was dreadful enough; even more macabre was the idea of Verney, at midnight and alone, entering that slippery and treacherous cavern, up to his shoulders in water perhaps, and trying to manhandle the corpse.

"It's far too dangerous," she protested. "You might fall and be drowned yourself. And anyway you wouldn't be able to see what you were doing."

"I've got to try, Harri. Don't you understand? It's no longer a question of protecting Richard from something he'd be happier not to know. This is far worse. When Henchman's body is discovered there will have to be an inquest, and any papers found on him will be put in as evidence. If Mrs. Sattle's statement is still legible, it will be read out in open court for all the world to hear."

9

On the day after the storm the Theo Capels had
an engagement to dine at the Hall. Because there
was no real friendliness between the sisters-in-law,
these invitations to each other's houses were issued
with meticulous politeness and always accepted.

Harriet was of course included in the party. Three
months earlier the prospect of spending several hours
in Verney's company would have made her wild
with delight. Last week it would have been a
dreaded embarrassment. But on this grey August
evening, as she brushed her short hair and tied her
blue sash with an abstraction that amounted almost
to blindness, she was wondering only whether the
could get him alone for long enough to talk him
out of his dangerous midnight expedition to the Grotto.

The broken glass in the cupola had been replaced
for the time being by boards and sacking, so they
were ushered into a hall that looked unusually
sombre and gloomy. Louisa glanced at the stacked
pictures and clicked her tongue; Harriet decided
that she was mentally blaming Julia for the thunderstorm.

The only person in the red anteroom was Verney, standing in front of the empty hearth. His
face seemed somehow older and he had sleepless
rings under his eyes.

"Ah, Verney!" began Louisa. "I am glad to find
you here, for I have a bone to pick with you."

Harriet guessed what sort of a bone it was going to be, so she immediately asked the Rector about
the ornaments that were displayed in a glass-fronted

cabinet facing the window. Through his painstaking replies she could hear Verney saying: "I am unable to get in touch with the—the person you are interested in. I have tried very hard, but with no success."

"It is extremely vexatious."

The Rector abandoned the cabinet and asked his wife: "Are you enlisting Verney's help with one of your good works, my dear?"

"Yes, you might certainly call it a very good work," she said with great satisfaction.

Harriet was disturbed by her thick-skinned indifference to the happiness of people she was supposed to be fond of. What sort of an obsession could have so completely destroyed her sense of proportion?

Julia came in, with a graceful, insincere aplogy for not having been there to greet her guests. She wore a corn-coloured silk dress, and her dark hair was parted in the middle, à la Madonna. Although she looked rather tired there was still a veiled and subdued sparkle about her; she would always be an enchantress. Louisa was reckoned a pretty woman, but against Julia's romantic beauty her healthy pink and white, her china-blue eyes and her cerise crepe dress looked merely commonplace.

"Why, you've had poor Catherine's topaz brooch reset," she exclaimed.

"Yes, isn't it improved?" said Julia, sweetly ignoring the note of criticism.

The family assembled and they moved into the dining room. Harriet found herself seated next to Sir Richard and opposite Louisa.

He began at once to thank her for her help in salvaging his pictures. "They were all so carefully

149

dried, not a mark on any of them. I am exceedingly grateful to you."

"Oh, that was nothing," she said, rather pleased all the same. "It was Verney's quickness and good sense that saved your pictures, sir."

"How fortunate that Verney happened to be on the spot," remarked Louisa. "For I collect that Julia had not the least idea what ought to be done. Well, why should she, after all? She is not accustomed to living in a treasure-house like Wardley."

"Julia had her hands full in the nursery," said Richard, "pacifying a delicate child and a superstitious old woman—for Nurse was completely beside herself, crying and moaning, which had a very bad effect on Ned. His nerves have been so much agitated that Julia decided he should stay in bed today; she has been reading to him the whole afternoon."

He gazed admiringly at his wife as she sat between his brothers at the far end of the table. He was intensely conscious of her unfailing care for Ned, whose health had always been such an anxiety. Everything Julia did was perfect. Louisa pursed up her mouth but said no more.

She and I, thought Harriet, and Verney and Julia; we are each hugging a secret—a different part of the same secret—how can we sit here tamely eating our dinner as though nothing is wrong? A fricasse of sweetbreads and a dish of chicken patties were removed with a saddle of mutton and some braised pigeons; Smethurst and his minions padded discreetly behind their chairs, and the children talked endlessly about the storm.

A lot of damage had been done: there were trees down everywhere, banks subsiding and gardens awash. Dick thought it was all a great lark.

"You might not think so," observed his father, "if you had lost your only apple tree and all your winter vegetables, with perhaps a few pullets who were to have supplied you with eggs for a whole year."

"But you'll make up all the things the villagers have lost, Papa," said Chloe. "You always do."

"And would you be satisfied with that, if you were in their shoes? Would you be content to see all the fruits of your hard work destroyed, so long as you could live on charity? Don't you think it's a bad thing for any man to lose his independence?"

Dick and Chloe quite plainly did not know what he was talking about. Studying their blank faces, he looked baffled and a little sad, and Harriet was reminded of something Verney had once said to her: "Richard takes such an exalted view of human destiny that he can make no allowance for human frailty."

Julia said: "If you are ready, Louisa? We'll leave the men to their wine."

This was a signal for Miss Pringle and the children to retire upstairs. When they had gone, Julia took Louisa and Harriet into the music room, where she chose to sit mostly in the evenings. The white drawing room, with its two fireplaces and glittering chandelier, was a little intimidating.

Julia's harp was draped in long shadows against the wall. The pianoforte had been opened, and the candles lit.

"Harriet," said Louisa, "I dare say Lady Capel would like to hear the Haydn sonata you have been practising."

"Yes, indeed," said Julia. "That would be delightful."

Harriet sat down at the pianoforte. She was quite

151

sure that Julia did not want to hear her stumbling through a piece of music that was much too difficult for her, but anything was better than having to make conversation in her present frame of mind. In fact, she soon realised that neither of the ladies was paying the slightest attention to her, so she was able to strum away softly to herself, while listening, inevitably, to their distinctly barbed conversation.

". . . you must find it very dull, buried here in the depths of the country," Louisa was saying.

"Not at all. The life we lead at Wardley suits me admirably."

"I am glad to hear it. I had an idea that you might have been happier in—let us say—Bath."

There was a short pause, as though Julia was a chess player working out her next move. When she spoke, she achieved a cool note of mockery.

"You seem to have got a very odd notion of my character, Louisa. I detest being mewed up in a city during the summer."

"There are some pleasant spots in the neighbourhood of Bath. The village of Widcombe, for instance. I believe you once lived in Widcombe Crescent?"

"I—I don't know who can have told you that." There was still an attempt at lightness, but it was not convincing. The blood had rushed away from Julia's face, and her skin was as pale as parchment.

Out of the corner of her eye Harriet saw the door open as Verney came into the music room. He came over to the pianoforte.

"I escaped as soon as I could. Theo was starting to talk about tithes."

Harriet made a slight motion with her hand, and jerked her head in the direction of the two women seated near the window. Verney took the hint; he too began to listen.

"You have many acquaintances there, have you not?"

"In Bath? Why should I?"

"I was under the impression that this protégé of yours, the drawing master—what's his name? Vincent? Does he not come from Bath?"

Harriet was startled. Not because Louisa had dragged in the painter—given her state of mind, she was bound to weave suspicions round anyone who lived in Bath, and it was all guesswork; she had not heard Mrs. Sattle describe Julia's lover. But Harriet had, and she began to make some hasty comparisons. Tall, dark, more than thirty years of age, plainly dressed, probably short of money. . . .

"Could it be?" whispered Verney. His mind was moving in the same direction, but he had not met John Vincent.

"It is possible," she admitted reluctantly.

Could this be why Julia had come back into the West Country? To rejoin her lover? She had certainly wasted no time in introducing John Vincent into her husband's house.

Harriet was appalled. She had been so anxious to protect Julia, it was largely thanks to her that Henchman was imprisoned in the Grotto. When his body was found there was a real danger that Verney might be charged with manslaughter, if not with murder. It would be unbearable to find out now that Julia had been John Vincent's mistress all along.

She was not at all reassured by the sight of Julia herself, apparently paralysed out of her senses, sitting stiffly on her sofa with a meaningless smile pinned to her mouth.

"It was a mistake to bring your artist friend here," Louisa was saying. "Besides being a great impertinence. Wardley Hall is not Widcombe Crescent."

"Would you care to explain that remark?" asked a voice from the doorway.

Richard had come in very quietly. As he stood coldly surveying them, a curiously menacing figure, Harriet felt a quiver of apprehension run up her spine.

"There is nothing to explain!" protested Julia. "Louisa objects to my choice of a painting master for Chloe, that is all. But this need not concern you, Richard. What does it matter if she has got hold of some—some foolish gossip and jumped to the wrong conclusion?"

Her voice was dreadfully unsteady.

"It matters to me." Richard walked over to the window. He looked down at Julia, deeply concerned. "Louisa has been attacking you, in vague terms, ever since we were married. If she has now come out with a definite accusation, it must be answered. We cannot allow this to go by default."

"Richard—please," whispered Julia on a note of real anguish. She was trembling painfully.

Harriet gazed at Richard with a horrified fascination. So besottedly in love with his wife that he had not the remotest idea what she was afraid of. (Such an exalted view of human destiny that he can make no allowances for human frailty . . . That was the trouble.)

Theo had come into the room behind his brother. He did his best to act as a peacemaker. "Let us not make mountains out of molehills. Louisa spoke without any real knowledge of the facts—"

"I did nothing of the kind!" Louisa jumped up, full of nervous energy and bad temper. Her face and neck had become hot and florid; the ugly red clashed with the bright pink of her dress. "I am not afraid of finding out the truth or speaking it. I can tell you some facts you none of you dared to discover about the life Julia was leading before you married her, Richard. I can quote chapter and verse—"

"That's a lie, to start with!" broke in Verney. "You haven't a shred of evidence."

"I don't need any," retorted Louisa. "She's guilty, there's no doubt of that. You only have to look at her."

Julia was weeping silently, her face white and tragic.

Richard put his hand on her shoulder. "Oh, my love—don't. I am so sorry."

"Have you gone mad?" cried Louisa, scornfully. "Can you not see, even now, what sort of a fool she has made of you? How much longer are you going on wilfully blinding yourself, protecting her?"

"No one is protecting her." Richard swung round, his voice suddenly harsh. "It is Julia who is heroically trying to protect me."

There was a moment of sheer incomprehension. Into it Louisa's gasp ended in a ridiculous squeak. *"You?* I don't understand—"

Richard faced his family. He had moved forward so that he now stood a little in front of Julia, who was practically hidden from them as he spoke.

"I don't know how much of the story you have managed to scavenge, Louisa. You seem to be aware that Julia once spent some months at a house in Widcombe Crescent, where she was frequently visited by a man she described as her cousin, though the landlady was pretty certain he was no such thing. Well, I was that ambiguous cousin, and if

Henchman had kept his accomplice waiting a little longer outside our gates, she would certainly have recognised me."

They were like waxworks: Louisa gaping and incredulous, the Rector's face full of foreboding, and Verney, leaning against the pianoforte, and half slewed round to stare at Richard as the impact of that announcement caught him unawares. The room was perfectly still, except for the flame of one candle, that was fluttering in a faint draught from the window. Harriet saw everything crystallised with the precise yet dreamlike clarity of her own astonishment.

"I cannot believe it," said Louisa. "You have invented this tale—to preserve her reputation . . ." The words faded away, for even Louisa had to recognise that this must be nonsense.

"But surely," protested Verney, "this happened three years ago? And you met Julia for the first time in April."

Richard shot him a brief glance. "I have known Julia since the summer of 1808. When she arrived at Bell Cottage this spring, we had already agreed to meet as strangers. In fact we set out deliberately to deceive you."

"You must not blame Richard for that." Julia got up and stood beside her husband, taking his arm. She had stopped crying and was now fairly composed, though her voice was husky. "Anything he did that was—not quite honourable, he did for my sake. So that I could marry him without becoming an object of speculation and rumour."

"And also for the children," added Richard. "I wanted them to love and value their stepmother as she deserved, without being misled by prejudice, and by feelings of resentment over something they are too young to understand."

"The summer of 1808," repeated Louisa flatly, "Catherine was still alive." She rounded on her husband. "It's your duty to reprove sin, isn't it? What are you going to say to this pair of licenced adulterers?"

"Louisa, they are married—"

"That's what I said—licenced! They tricked you into it. If you'd known the truth—"

"I did know," said the Rector. "Richard insisted on telling me everything before I performed the ceremony."

This, for Louisa, was the final straw.

"You mean to tell me you condoned their wickedness!" she almost screamed at him. "Allowing them to marry—"

"My good Louisa, he had no choice!" exclaimed Verney. "He's obliged to marry his parishioners when they ask him to. And the more they stand in need of it, the better he ought to be pleased."

This last piece of elegant moralising was heard only by Harriet, for Louisa was still in full spate.

"You forced me to go to the wedding, to sit there in church and watch him making those blasphemous promises to his whore. . . ."

"This has gone far enough!" said Richard sharply. "I'm sorry, Theo, but you will have to stop her."

Theo was quite incapable of stopping Louisa, who had now begun to sob out wild and totally disjointed phrases in a hoarse monotone.

"I thought you were so good . . . I only wanted to serve you, I never asked . . . a pure and disinterested love . . . while all the time this vile, filthy conspiracy . . . Oh, it's too horrible . . ."

Her relations seemed completely bewildered by

this outburst. Harriet alone perceived the exact moment at which Louisa stopped abusing her husband and started on her brother-in-law.

She emerged from behind the pianoforte and advanced on Louisa, saying: "Come, Mrs. Theo! You should not be carrying on in this fashion, it's not at all the thing, and you will feel very uncomfortable tomorrow when you remember what you have been saying."

As she heard herself talking in this bright, governessy way, she was convinced that they must all recognise her as the most complete fraud, but when she seized Louisa by the elbow she was surprised and relieved to meet with no resistance. Louisa allowed herself to be propelled towards a door at the end of the music room which led into the small drawing room beyond.

In the midst of her preoccupation she saw the rest of the Capels. The three men embarrassed by Louisa's display, and Julia, generally so competent, too stunned by her own emotions to do anything useful. Verney was the most self-possesed; he held open the door for them.

The small drawing room was the place where the coin collection was kept. Louisa stumbled into the very chair in which Miss Nixon had sheltered from the thunderstorm—was it only yesterday? It seemed a century ago. The storm in Louisa's mind was smouldering fiercely; she sat tearing at her handkerchief and repeating under her breath: "How could you do it? How could you?"

Harriet, watching her, wondered why she had never realised that Louisa was secretly and hopelessly in love with Sir Richard. This explained so many things about her that that explanation itself hardly ranked as a surprise.

But then nothing could seem very surprising against the revelation that three years ago Sir Richard had been Julia's secret lover.

Verney came into the room, full of solicitude. "Is there anything you want, Harri? That I can do?"

"Just try to keep your brother out of here if you can. Both your brothers."

10

Half an hour later Theo, Louisa and Harriet were driven back to the Parsonage, being seen off at the front door by Verney, who had been left alone to do the honours, for Richard and Julia had disappeared.

Louisa was reasonably calm, though her heart was still pumping hard, and her face was blotched and swollen. Her companions supported and encouraged her. Verney was impressed with the way Harriet had risen to the occasion: firm and sensible yet kind, she was the only person who had entirely kept her head. He would have liked a few words with her, but was too busy getting Louisa off the premises before she made a scene in front of the servants.

He was standing in the hall, rather at a loss, when he saw Richard coming towards him down the grand staircase.

Richard caught sight of him and paused. "Have they gone?"

"Yes."

"I shall have to talk to you if you please."

"Very well."

They went into the library. There was a barrier of awkwardness between them, through which neither could look at the other. Richard contemplated his elegant calf bindings, smooth leather and gold leaf gleaming gently in the lamplight. Verney gazed at the bust of Socrates. He could not think of anything to say.

"Was it you who put Henchman in the Grotto?" asked Richard at last.

"My God—Henchman! Have they found the body?"

"Set your mind at rest. There is no body. I let him out yesterday afternoon, just as the water was starting to rise."

"You did? Well, of all the—how did you happen to be there?"

"I was following him. What I want to know, Verney, is how did you happen to be there? That little brute didn't know who his assailant was, but he described you to the life and claimed that you were an emissary from Louisa."

"I am sure you found no difficulty in believing him. I expect you think I was in league with her to ruin your wife—"

"I never thought anything of the kind."

"Didn't you?" asked Verney, doubtfully. "I know you have not forgiven me yet for trying to warn you against Julia. Of course, if I'd known the true facts of the case I'd have kept my mouth shut. As it is, I have been very conscious of your resentment ever since I came home—"

"But this is absolute nonsense," interrupted Richard. "I assure you, I haven't the smallest feeling of resentment—I never did have, from the moment I recovered my temper and considered how far I had wilfully misled you. There has certainly been a degree of reserve since your return—I have not not been able to feel at ease with you—but this

160

was entirely a matter of my own guilty conscience. I knew I had treated you abominably, yet it still seemed impossible to tell you so."

"Oh," said Verney, very much taken aback. He appreciated that there must be a number of unexpected items on Richard's conscience, but he had not so far considered himself as one of them.

"Perhaps I can now make you understand why I became so excessively angry. It was when you compared Julia with Pamela Sutcliffe."

"Well, I am not surprised. It was very uncivil of me, and I beg your pardon. There was not the smallest resemblance between them."

"Oh yes, there was, even if you didn't know it at the time. Pamela had been your mistress and Julia had been mine. That was what I could not bear to remember." Richard began to walk about the library in a very agitated way. "I was obsessed by the injury I had done her. She was a perfectly innocent girl when I seduced her; to me she seems, and always will seem, innocent still. Yet you apparently recognised something in her character that made you suspicious and contemptuous—"

"But my dear Richard, you are refining too much on a metaphysical question that is quite beyond my powers of discernment! I simply thought that Julia was acting a part, and I was right. Only I mistook the part she was acting. I assumed that she did not really care for you and was merely pretending to do so, while in fact she already cared so much that she felt obliged to dissemble her true sentiments—it was the suggestion of something artificial that put me on my guard."

"I never thought of that!" exclaimed Richard. He stood lost in a cloud of anxious musing and remorse, until he was brought down to earth by Smethurst, who came in looking portentous.

"Could you inform me, sir," enquired the butler, "where her ladyship would wish me to set the tea table?"

The ritual pouring out and drinking of tea was of course the climax of the evening in every well-bred household, especially when there were visitors. No one who came to dinner ever left before tea, it was unheard of. However, the Theo Capels had done just that, and poor Smethurst, as he hunted for the remaining members of the family through a string of deserted reception rooms, didn't know what the world was coming to.

His master made matters worse by saying casually, "We shan't want any tea this evening, Smethurst. You might bring in a bottle of brandy."

"Very well, sir," said Smethurst, disapprovingly.

Richard had recovered sufficiently to wink at Verney, and as soon as the old man was out of the room they lapsed, like schoolboys, into a fit of stifled laughter. After which they felt much better.

A few minutes later, sipping his brandy, Verney felt able to ask: "Where did you first meet Julia?"

"I found her standing at the side of the Bath Road on the second of June, 1808, looking like an angel in distress. Is that even worse than you supposed? It was an eminently proper occasion, in fact a tragic one, for she had her father with her and he was a very sick man—he died a month later."

"He was a parson, wasn't he?"

"He was in orders, though he never held a benefice. He had private means, and spent his life reading and writing on various historical subjects; he published a couple of books and belonged to several learned societies. They lived just outside Scarborough, and in a very good style, I imagine. Mr. Johnson was a savant but not a recluse, and they entertained liberally. Julia was their only child. Her mother died when she was seventeen, so from then on she was her father's housekeeper and hostess. They had been settled in this way for about five years when Mr. Johnson suffered an apoplectic stroke. The physical signs did not remain very long, and it was some time before Julia realised that her father's mind had been affected in a most unfortunate way: he had become completely unreliable over money. He was speculating wildly, buying up property, running up debts. . . . She tried to restrain him, but he would not listen; his temper had become very violent, and he succeeded in quarrelling with all the old friends who gave him sound advice, while turning to a set of people who callously exploited his foolishness. Eventually things reached such a pass that Julia was warned to take everything she could out of the house before they had the duns in. She sold her mother's jewellery, hired a post-chaise and set out with her father for Bath. By now he had made himself ill and was ready to seek advice."

"Why Bath? Wouldn't Harrogate or Buxton have been more convenient?"

"It was the usual pathetic story; she'd heard of some wonderful doctor down there who had an infallible cure for her father's condition. She had a wretched journey with the old man; he was behaving very oddly, yet he didn't look either ill enough or mad enough to excuse his eccentricities, so there were continual difficulties. When I came across them, three miles outside of Bath, he had just accused the post boys of trying to steal his dressing case. He was actually belabouring one of them with his stick. I must admit," said Richard, reaching for the decanter, "that there was something extremely comic about the whole business, it was like a scene from one of Fielding's novels. If it hadn't been for the despairing look in Julia's eyes. . . . Well, I offered my assistance, and succeeded in pacifying the post boys. Having learnt where they were bound for, I drove behind them to the house in Beaufort Square where Julia had written for lodgings. It was just as well I did, for Mr. Johnson immediately insulted the landlady, and if I hadn't brought a little pressure to bear—and flourished my title in a remarkably vulgar way—I doubt if she'd have taken them in. I felt so concerned for them both that I returned a week later to see how they were getting on. The old man was now extremely ill, he'd had another seizure, and she was nursing him night and day without rest. I told her she ought to hire a woman to help her, and she burst into tears and said she couldn't afford to. That was when she began to tell me their whole history. She was thankful to have someone to confide in. She was devoted to her father, who had been a man of great abilities and an excellent disposition; the pain of watching that terrible change had been almost unbearable. I suppose we were conscious of a certain affinity, for I too—" Richard broke off rather suddenly, and Verney completed the sentence for him.

"You also had a most unreasonable invalid on your hands. I've never heard you breathe a word against Catherine, but we all know she led you a dog's life, those last few years."

"My poor little Kate," said Richard softly. "She was so gay and pretty, she wasn't designed to bear the weight of affliction. Some people haven't the strength."

Verney thought of Catherine, thin and sickly, her good looks destroyed, lying on a sofa incessantly complaining. Nobody knew what she had to endure, her grinding headaches, her nervous palpitations; nobody ever came near her, they were all so selfish and Richard was the worst of the lot. Whatever he tried to do for her comfort or diversion, she was never quite satisfied. He ought to have done something different. Richard had borne all this with the most exemplary patience, sitting for hours beside her sofa, humouring her querulous demands, reading to her, trying to arouse her interest in something other than her own health. He had been a paragon among husbands. Did it really make any difference to know that at the same time he had been slipping over to Bath to visit Julia?

"Henry Johnson's symptoms were far more distressing," continued Richard. "Mercifully he didn't live long after the second seizure. Then it was a question of what was to become of Julia. She had a little money left, not a great deal, and she was afraid that everything else they possessed would be divided among the creditors. In spite of this, it sounded to me as though the house itself had originally been part of a settlement on her mother that must descend to Julia. She did not want to deal with her father's lawyer, who had become one of his most rapacious creditors, so I persuaded her to let me turn over the entire legal proceedings to Coverdale; I knew he would see that she got everything she was entitled to.

"I also prevailed on her to stay where she was for the time being, not in Beaufort Square, which was airless and noisy in the heat of the summer;

165

I found her a much pleasanter lodging in Widcombe, where she could rest and recuperate. She was very lonely, and I got into the habit of visiting her pretty often. I had just been elected to the committee of the Bath and West Society and was very much occupied with calling on landowners and farmers in Wiltshire and Somerset, on behalf of the Society, so it was easy for me to be constantly in Bath. Of course I shouldn't have gone near her. It was a wicked and irresponsible way to behave."

"I don't see that," objected Verney. "You were trying to help her. You didn't foresee how it would turn out."

"Didn't I? Perhaps not. Yet from the moment she moved to Widcombe Crescent I became wonderfully discreet; I told Julia we had better pretend to be cousins, and I always went to the house on foot; I didn't want anyone to recognise the crest on the curricle."

"Well, it stands to reason, you would not wish to start a lot of talk. Mrs. Sattle was quite taken in; she never guessed she had been entertaining a baronet unawares. She thought you must be very short of funds."

"Oh, you've seen old Sattle, have you? What else did she say?"

One thing she had said flashed through Verney's memory with a shocking clarity. Hastily banishing the pagan images, he searched around for something more suitable.

"She said you were quite the gentleman and might have taken any girl's fancy—in spite of your poverty-stricken appearance. I'm afraid she does not think much of your tailor."

Richard might have gone to Widcombe Crescent

on foot; he had certainly not gone in disguise, and it was amusing to discover the effect created by his exquisitely cut coats and pantaloons, their severe simplicity of line, the complete absence of foppery and fancy waistcoats.

"I was never one of your Milsom Street beaux." Richard's eyes lit up with a secret amusement, and Verney wondered what he was remembering.

"We were very happy," he said. "At first. A great and lasting passion is sometimes compared to a kind of madness, but that is a false analogy. You live in a world that is governed by a beautiful and ordered sanity, like the music of the sphere. It's when you try to reconcile this with the world outside that you are driven mad. Julia is at heart very serious and good, she was haunted by the wrong she felt she was doing to Catherine, and nothing I could say—however, there's no need to go into all that. We decided to separate."

"Mrs. Sattle thought there were disagreements over money."

"So there were. I wanted to make some provision for her, and she wouldn't let me. Fortunately Coverdale had dealt very successfully with old Johnson's affairs, and there was more saved from the wreck than we had expected. Julia decided to go and live with her friend Mrs. Williams, who had offered her a home in Cheshire. She did not wish to return to Scarborough.

"We said good-bye. It was February two years ago, we had known each other for eight months, and for six of them we had been in love. I came back here and looked at my guns. It would have been so easy to go out, alone with a dog, and have an accident. But the children needed me, and so did poor Catherine in her way, so I just went on existing from hour to hour. I had promised Julia not to write. I never expected to see her again."

And we none of us guessed, thought Verney, marvelling at his brother's extraordinary fortitude. He had kept his own counsel and fulfilled his obligations so well that no one doubted the sincerity of his grief, ten months later, when Catherine died of a putrid fever which she had caught from one of the maids, and which proved fatal to her weakened constitution. And certainly the grief had been sincere; he had been happy with Catherine once, and he had a great capacity for affection, for compassion. Even so. . . .

"I suppose Catherine's death changed verything?"

"I broke my promise and wrote to Julia a week after the funeral, asking her to marry me as soon as I was out of mourning. At first she refused; she had so many ridiculous scruples why she ought not to marry me that it took me the whole of my mourning year to get rid of them. When she finally came round, we still had to solve the problem of how and where we were to meet and fall in love."

"I don't see that there was any great problem in that."

"Don't you? Bearing in mind that our previous association was a deadly secret, that we lived in different parts of the kingdom, and that we hadn't a single acquaintance in common? I suppose we could have arranged an encounter in the public assembly rooms of some watering place. That would not have done at all. You must remember that one of my chief objects has been to make Julia acceptable to Kitty and Chloe. If they were unable to love or respect my second wife, I think the character of each might be seriously affected, though in different ways."

Verney was silent, trying to work out how a man of their position in society generally met his future wife. Very often he'd known her all his life; she was the daughter of a neighbour, or a family connection. She might be the sister of one of his friends —or the friend of one of his sisters, perhaps that was the most popular equation of all. And if you belonged to the right set, there were always country house parties and London balls where the hostesses spent their time manoeuvring unattached young ladies into the orbit of eligible men. Only it seemed that Julia did not know any of these hostesses, and it was imposible to enter the charmed circle without the right sponsors. A country neighbourhood was perhaps the only place where people of respectable birth could meet naturally and freely, even when they belonged to rather different worlds and where there was a wide disparity of fortune. It would have looked extremely strange if Richard had gone running off to Cheshire, but for Julia to come to Wardley, with Bell Cottage standing empty—the temptation was obvious.

"All that stuff about Bowyer's mother, I suppose there wasn't a word of truth in it?"

"I'm afraid that was part of our scheme for getting Julia accepted. We knew Bowyer couldn't be reached, so it seemed safe enough."

"You deliberately made fools of us," said Verney, with his first real sense of grievance, as he remembered several misleading episodes which in retrospect were positively humiliating.

"Yes, and I am extremely sorry," said Richard. "Console yourself with the fact that we made fools of ourselves also. We were not such successful deceivers as we imagined; I showed my partiality much too clearly and much too soon, while Julia dissembled hers in such a way that you found her insincere. I think we had seen ourselves acting out our parts in front of a docile audience whom we could easily carry along with us; instead we had the sort of audience who wanted to hiss the play, or even to jump on the stage and join in—"

"Louisa, for instance?"

"And you too, Verney. At the Southbury Ball when you wanted to dance with Julia all evening."

Just my luck, thought Verney bitterly, trying to philander with the girl who was secretly engaged to my brother.

"I didn't care a straw whether she liked me or not," he announced loftily. "I mean—that is to say —I had no serious intentions."

"Of course not," said the new Richard he had not yet got used to. "You simply wanted an agreeable flirtation with a girl who was quite old enough to know jest from earnest. But from our standpoint, what a contemptible creature I saw myself to be, exposing Julia to such an approach from her future brother-in-law. Why, you might even have fallen in love with her. She was anxious for you to like her, but when I pointed out the dangers, her manner towards you froze, and of course you began to think she was a calculating schemer. It was mostly our dislike of this double dealing which made us hurry on with our pretended courtship at such a rate—and that gave everybody an excuse to shake their heads and talk about my being infatuated. Even so, I think we should have lived down our mistakes with no questions asked, if Louisa hadn't brought Henchman into our midst."

"She didn't do that, Richard. It was Henchman who wrote to her."

"Yes, but she'd given him the original incentive

to come into Wiltshire. Is it possible you don't know who he is?"

"An attorney's clerk, according to Mrs. Sattle."

"Exactly. He was one of Coverdale's clerks."

"Our Mr. Coverdale? That's been the family man of business since the Wars of the Roses or thereabouts? Good God!"

"He was an underling who has recently been dismissed, I collect, for a peccadillo in the office. Three years ago Coverdale sent him down to Bath with some papers for Julia to sign, connected with the sale of her house in Yorkshire. He knew nothing of the business in hand, nor how she came to be a client of the firm; he simply acted as a messenger. It appears that he also made friends with Mrs. Sattle and discovered from her that Miss Johnson had a lover. A few months ago Louisa wrote to Coverdale, suggesting that he might be able to unearth some discreditable details about Julia which would prevent our marriage. Even Louisa hesitated to ask me if I would frank this particular letter, so it was opened in the outer office, where Henchman read it before it was taken in to the holy of holies. Coverdale replied—but I dare say you saw his reply?"

"I heard that he had snubbed Louisa. I take it that he knows—"

"I've never told him in so many words, but he must have guessed. Anyway, Coverdale himself is as safe as the tomb. How safe you can judge, from the fact that when Henchman read the letter he entirely missed the point. He simply assumed that Miss Johnson, three years after her indiscretion in Bath, was about to marry a man she had only just met, and who also happened to be one of Coverdale's numerous clients. Still he made no move. I

171

don't believe that he has ever before tried extortion on the grand scale. It's a little too dangerous. But he told me yesterday that he's been turned off, he wouldn't say exactly why, and it's of no consequence except that desperation made him bold enough to come down here and try his luck at threatening a woman who had never done him any harm."

"There's one thing I can't make out," began Verney.

"Why didn't Julia tell me straight away?"

"Yes. That's what worried me most; the definite proof (as it seemed to me) that she'd deceived you. But considering that you knew all about Widcombe Crescent—well, of course you did," said Verney, becoming slightly confused. "I mean you were there. So why didn't she get you to send Henchman packing without more ado?"

"It's a little hard to explain. I told you that Julia had a great many scruples about our marriage. Absurd, all of them, but such prominence is always given to the benefits of rank and wealth, and it cannot be very pleasant always to be taking, even from someone you love. And besides Julia is very conscious of having been the unwilling cause of a great deal of dissension in the family. I think this has been preying on her mind. When Henchman appeared on the scene, demanding money, she simply did not want to come to me about this sordid reminder of our disreputable past. She wanted to settle it alone. She was anxious to spare me pain, and I think it was also a matter of pride, poor girl."

"Yes, I can understand that," said Verney slowly.

"Henchman wanted five hundred pounds, or he'd come to me with Mrs. Sattle's account of Julia's residence in Widcombe Crescent. Julia's first instinct was to pay; then she discovered that she couldn't get hold of the money without my knowing, and she had also begun to see that it was ridiculous to pay such a price, simply to save me from being reminded of something I was hardly likely to forget. She had one more shot in her locker, and that didn't cost a penny. She wrote Henchman a sharp reply, saying that his story was an impudent fabrication and if he wasn't careful he'd be thrown into gaol. She heard no more from him, and concluded that she'd successfully scared him away. It never dawned on her that he might be hawking his information round the family. She was upset and nervous, all the same; I knew there was something wrong, though I couldn't make out what, and two nights ago I dragged the whole story out of her. I wasn't as sanguine as Julia; it seemed incredible that anyone possessed of such an excellent piece of scandal should give up so tamely. Yesterday I rode over to Southbury in search of Henchman. They told me at the inn that he'd gone out in a hired gig. I hunted him down, with wearisome persistence, until I came to my own back gate. The rain was falling in torrents and there wasn't a soul in sight, but I could see the marks where a carriage had stood for some time, just inside the drive, and some signs of scuffling on the grass, smears of mud, as though a body had been dragged down the steps; I went into the Grotto and there I found my man, bound and gagged and exceedingly frightened. And now, for God's sake, Verney, take pity on my curiosity. Why did you put him in the Grotto?"

Verney told him.

Richard listened in growing amazement.

"My dear fellow, this is coals of fire indeed! That

173

you should struggle so hard and so ingeniously on my behalf, and after I had treated you so badly. I don't know what to say. Except that I an uncommonly grateful."

"My efforts didn't accomplish anything. They weren't even necessary."

"They might have been. That's what counts."

The door opened slightly, and Julia's voice said: "Richard? Oh, I didn't know—I thought you were alone."

Both men jumped to their feet.

"You must come in here at once, my love," said Richard, "and thank Verney for the way he has been fighting our battles in the last few days. I think you will be very much surprised."

She came towards them, hesitant and plainly uncertain of herself. She looked unexpectedly fragile. Verney thought of her standing by the roadside while her half-crazy father tussled with the post boys. And of her crying her heart out, alone in the Widcombe lodging, after she had sent Richard away.

"Do you hate me more than ever?" she asked him in a low voice, "Now you know what a trouble I have been to Richard?"

"Hate you? What nonsense! It is only now that I know the whole story, I am able to wish you joy."

And he held out his hand to her.

"I call that very handsome of you. What did Richard mean about your fighting our battles?"

Richard began to tell her, and her eyes grew larger and brighter than ever.

"But Verney—why?" she asked at last. "You already distrusted me, you thought I was a perfidious hussy, and after meeting poor Mrs. Sattle you had every reason to think so. Of course you wanted to protect your brother—but surely you must have

174

felt that it was only a matter of time before I caused another scandal and made him wretchedly unhappy?"

"I was staking everything on the hope that there wouldn't be any more scandal. I thought you were in love with him. At least, Harriet said so, and she talked me into agreeing with her."

"Harriet was right," said Julia.

"I must be very thick-witted," remarked Richard, "but I cannot imagine how Harriet came to be embroiled in this business."

"Neither can I," admitted Verney, "except that she is a most persistent girl, and once Louisa had shown her Henchman's letter, nothing would keep her out. In the end I was very glad of her support. And you need not be afraid that she will chatter or let out anything she shouldn't, as she was used to do, for I don't know how it is, she has entirely altered in the last few months. Did you not notice how good she was with Louisa this evening? She is so sensible now, as well as being very pretty. At least I think so."

Richard and Julia exchanged glances, but neither of them spoke.

"There's one thing that puzzles me," said Richard, after a slight pause. "Assuming that your suspicions had been justified, were you completely convinced that I should refuse to go on living with Julia if I ever found out? Did it not strike you that I might still love her as much as ever?"

Verney felt as though his feet had been kicked from under him. He had never considered anything so unexpected. Richard, who was so upright, so high-minded, so proud, so fastidious, so moral, so apt to sit in silent judgment on the antics of his disreputable brother—yes, but wait a moment, he was not nearly as moral as everyone supposed, and those silent judgments would have been either a matter of pure hypocrisy or, more likely, occasions of acute discomfort.

Richard was watching his face. "What an unconscionable prig you must have thought me."

It was hardly possible to say, yes I did. Verney said nothing at all.

"You are not to tease him, Richard," said Julia. "It's very ill-natured. And Verney has public opinion on his side. The majority of men, I think, would repudiate a woman who had lived with a lover before her marriage and then lied about it. You are an exception to rules of that sort, because you are both honest and generous, more able to forgive—"

"I hate that word."

"Yes, I'm afraid one always associates it with screwing up the most prodigious effort of will to do something repugnant—"

"Like forgiving Louisa. And I may as well tell you straight away that I shall not be able to bring myself—"

"Oh yes, you will: for Theo's sake. You cannot hurt Theo after he has been so uncondemning towards us. But we need not consider Louisa just now. If I had been unfaithful to you, I believe you would forgive me."

"I should not need to. I should simply go on loving you, that's the difference."

"My darling there is no difference!"

They were off on the sort of discussion that was clearly familiar to them. Verney wondered if he had been inhabiting a place where all the acknowledged landmarks were Gothic follies, unrelated to the real country of human love and human need.

He tried to test out Julia's philosophy. How

would he feel (for instance) if he found that some unprincipled brute had been making love to Harriet? Well, he'd thrash the fellow, make him sorry he was ever born, but of course nothing would really change his feeling for Harri. Which was odd, when you came to think of it. . . . Richard and Julia were still happily arguing, but he had stopped listening to them.

11 .

Harriet sat up with Louisa most of the night. The Rector had moved into his dressing room; Louisa sighed and cried and tossed in the big bed, unable to sleep, refusing the laudanum drops that had been poured for her. She had a compulsive need to talk.

"How could he enter into such a life of deceit? He was always so upright and honourable; I believed in him. I trusted him, he was my ideal of what a gentleman ought to be. . . ."

Ever since she was nineteen, apparently. Bit by bit the whole picture of her life emerged: Louisa Delamaine, the daughter of a Worcestershire squire, not rich though well-born. Anxious to marry as soon as she could—there were three younger sisters treading on her heels. Theo Capel had been a college friend of one of her brothers; he asked her to marry him after a fairly short acquaintance. She liked him better than any man she had yet seen, enough to make her accept his proposal and look forward confidently to a happy, useful future. She was then invited to Wardley Hall to meet his family —and before the end of the visit she had fallen hopelessly in love with Richard. What ought she

177

to have done? It was a dreadful predicament, Richard was a married man, entirely devoted to his pretty wife and their three small children—there was naturally no question of a love affair between him and Louisa, but should she have broken her engagement to his brother, in order to put herself out of danger? The awkwardness of doing such a thing, without being able to give a reason, was quite sufficient to daunt a conventional girl who did not at all wish to appear as a jilt. Besides, if she could not marry Richard, Louisa thought she could be a loyal wife to Theo while worshipping her idol in secret. And it seemed as though she had made a providential choice, for a year later Ned was born, and from then on Catherine became more and more of an invalid, so that Louisa was constantly required to help and advise her brother-in-law, until she gradually became a substitute lady of the manor. Their intimacy grew, in a perfectly innocent way, and she felt that she was giving him everything that a virtuous woman could give to a man who was not her husband. If her unruly desires sometimes made her feel restless and guilty, she crushed them down relentlessly telling herself that Richard was so noble and good, he would be shocked if he knew what was going on in her mind.

"I thought he'd be angry with me. What a fool I was, when all the time I suppose he would have made love to any woman who consented. He and that Jezebel, I can't bear to think of them together —but I wish I hadn't said all those things this evening in the music room. Do you think they guessed? That they are triumphing over me and sneering?"

"I am sure no one guessed," said Harriet.

After the humiliation of her own silly pursuit of

Verney, she had come to dislike, almost to hate Louisa, who had never stopped scolding and admonishing her, harping on and on about the fearful indelicacy, the contemptible weakness of a woman who wore her heart on her sleeve. Now she understood why. It was essential for Louisa herself to hide her love for Richard. Originally this secrecy had been a necessary safeguard, but since the arrival of Julia it had become a pathetic sop to her wounded pride. Tonight she lay as though she was on the rack, with her hair streaking damply round her tear-stained face, clinging to her pitiful secret and saying she would die if Richard ever found out.

Eventually she did get to sleep, and Harriet was able to steal away thankfully to her own bed for a few hours' rest. In the morning she told the maids not to disturb Mrs. Capel, saying she was a little indisposed, and after family prayers had been said she sat down alone to breakfast with the Rector.

He was also looking very tired, his pleasant face creased with a frown of preoccupation. He certainly hadn't the charm of the other two Capels, neither Sir Richard's dark splendour nor Verney's engaging liveliness, and it was easy to understand what had happened to Louisa, but the Rector was a kind man and Harriet felt very sorry for him. She thought he must be puzzled by the violence of his wife's distress when confronted by a family scandal, and tried, somewhat ineffectively, to make it seem less unreasonable.

"I think Mrs. Capel's nerves have been a good deal affected by the weather. Lots of people are made quite ill by thunder, I believe."

"I blame myself very much," said the Rector, not

179

attending to this well-meaning inanity. "I ought to have known what was going on. To negotiate with a common criminal for such a purpose—if I had got their permission to tell Louisa the whole story in the first place, we should have escaped that degradation. But it wouldn't have done. She was bound to hold any new wife of Richard's in the utmost aversion, at least until she had learnt to accept a rival, and it would have been madness to let her know the truth about him and Julia."

Harriet gave a slight gasp of surprise. He looked up, smiling rather sadly, and said: "My dear child, you don't have to pretend with me. You found out last night, did you not? I guessed as much from the kind way you tried to stop her talking too wildly, when we were coming home in the chaise. But I have always known the true nature of her affection for my brother."

"You have?"

"Well, since the year after our marriage. She is not to blame; she has never done anything wrong (until now, spurred on by her wretched jealousy) and my brother, needless to say, has never suspected for a moment—he is such a modest fellow, not a scrap of conceit about him. He has been puzzled and disappointed, all along, by Louisa's attitude towards Julia; I doubt if he is any nearer guessing the reason."

"Mr. Capel," said Harriet, uncertain how to put the question that had been troubling her, "do you think there is any likelihood of your wife's making the facts known—thinking it her duty, perhaps—"

"No, she will never do that. She was trying to cause trouble between husband and wife, hoping that this would actually lead to a separation, but even in those circumstances she would not have spread any public gossip about Julia. She has a great sense of family obligation. She has so many excellent qualities; I ought to have done more to help her withstand the evils of her situation. Even now, it is not too late."

Harriet was curiously touched by his gentle, uncritical stoicism. He is really a good man, she thought, a better man perhaps, than either of his brothers. But it doesn't make any difference; they are the ones that women fall in love with.

"Will you take a little more coffee, sir?"

He passed her his cup, looked round his bright, neat breakfast parlour, and said, "We shall have to get away from here. I ought to have made this decision as soon as my brother announced his engagement to Miss Johnson. Instead of sitting here while my poor Louisa got steadily more unhappy and exercised her ill-temper on anyone within sight —which I am afraid was very often you, Harriet. I am sorry your time with us has been so uncomfortable."

In her anxiety to reassure him Harriet began to say that she had enjoyed herself excessively. This was going rather too far. Hastily changing the subject, she asked what he would do if he left Wardley.

"An old friend of mine has recently been appointed to the see of Welhampton. One of the Canons' stalls there has just become vacant, and I believe I might be considered. There would be a house in the close, of course, and some congenial society."

"Are you acquainted with the Bishop's family?"

"Dr. Brassey is unmarried. He is a distinguished scholar, not very much up in the ways of the world."

This sounded excellent. Louisa would have plenty to occupy her mind. In six months' time she would probably be managing the Palace.

In spite of so many distractions, Harriet was still haunted by the threat of Henchman's body being discovered in the Grotto. Directly after breakfast she left the house and made for the lake, noticing as soon as she entered the pleasure grounds how far the water had receded. The Grotto must be accessible by now.

A voice hailed her from the battered and rather dejected-looking Rustic Bridge. Verney splashing his way through the puddles. She ran to meet him.

"I was coming to call on you," he said.

"The body? What's happened? Have they discovered it yet?"

"There isn't any body. Richard found Henchman and released him at the height of the storm, while you and I were being bored to death by Slingsby. He was obliged to let the fellow go free; you dare not take an extortioner to court, for fear of what might come out. But I reckon he won't show his face in these parts again, he didn't enjoy being tied up in the dark and Richard did not treat him too gently either. Imagine his fury with the villain who attempted to persecute Julia! They are so much in love, you know; what a fool I was to suppose that she might be deceiving him, when it's perfectly plain that they are hand in glove and always have been."

"I am surprised at Sir Richard." Harriet was pursuing her own train of thought. "I do not think he has behaved at all well."

"I am sorry," said Verney, becoming instantly solemn. "You have been so charitable about Julia, I hoped you could be able to include Richard in your charity. I expect you blame him for having led her astray. He feels it extremely, I assure you."

"I don't care which of them was led astray," said Harriet airily. "It's no business of mine. But I do think Sir Richard ought to have told you that he had rescued Henchman before the water rose, instead of leaving you in suspense for a whole night and a day. It was very thoughtless of him."

Verney gazed at her for a moment, and then began to laugh.

"So you think that's his worst crime, do you? Harri, he could not tell me. He had no certain means of knowing who had put Henchman into the Grotto, or why. We have all been at cross-purposes."

He began to give her a compressed account of everything he had heard from Richard the night before.

They wandered along the southern shore of the lake. The stormy weather had cleared, and it was a calm, bright September day, rather hot. The thick grass, still quite wet, was sparkling in the sun.

"So all our efforts were wasted," said Harriet.

They had stopped a little short of the small Gothic building called the Nunnery, and stood looking at the water, which had shrunk back inside its proper contours but was still churned-up and opaque. The banks were a sticky, chocolate brown. Only the swans, sailing by, looked immaculate and unconcerned.

"Not wasted," said Verney. "I thought that at first, but it's not so. All this trouble in the family has taught me so much about you that I didn't know before. You have been such a tower of strength, Harri—and so wise, too, for you have said all along that whatever Julia may have done, she isn't a cheat or a deceiver. Why, I might have gone tale-

183

bearing to Richard and set him against me for ever, if you hadn't stopped me. I don't know where I should have been without you."

"You told me that I was too interfering, and that I should end up as bad as Louisa," she pointed out objectively.

"I dare say I shall always tell you things like that from time to time. You won't take them to heart, will you, my darling?"

Harriet gazed at him mutely, unable to answer.

Verney caught her by the shoulder and tilted her face up towards him. Her bonnet got in the way, so she took it off.

Presently he stopped kissing her to ask: "You do love me, don't you?"

"I thought everybody in the countryside knew that."

"Oh, Harri, don't," he exclaimed with a groan of remorse. "How wicked of me to treat you in that heartless way, trading on your innocence—I deserve to be shot!"

He pressed his face against her shoulder. Harriet dropped her bonnet on the grass in order to run her fingers through his strong brown hair. He started telling her how happy they were going to be, he would make up for the past, he would take care of her—

"Are we going to be married before any of these charming things happen?"

"Of course we are, you silly goose. At least—"

"What's the matter now?"

"How can I ask you to marry me? I haven't enough money."

"That doesn't signify. I've got plenty."

"My dear girl, you know very well how much it

signifies. Your trustees will never allow you to marry a man in my situation."

"Well, if you are going to back out a second time, I warn you I shall have hysterics," said Harriet, brazenly encouraging him to kiss her again.

At this juncture Sir Richard and Lady Capel appeared, walking towards them round the corner of the Nunnery.

Both couples were petrified into a state of acute embarrassment. The obvious cause—that Harriet and Verney were apparently enjoying an amorous romp —was quite put in the shade by the general consciousness that this was the first encounter since that scene in the music room, between Richard and Julia and the eighteen-year-old girl who knew so much about them that they would rather have kept hidden. Harriet and Verney could imagine what they must be feeling, and were equally tongue-tied.

Then Harriet was inspired to be deliberately outrageous.

"Lady Capel, will you please tell me what I ought to do? Verney is flirting with me again, and he won't marry me because I have trustees."

Her inspiration worked; the spell was broken.

"How very faint-hearted of Verney," said Julia, smiling. "I am sure Richard can strengthen his resolution."

"Do you really want to marry my scamp of a brother, Harriet?" enquired Richard. "Verney, you are a lucky man. I congratulate you."

"Can none of you understand? I'm not in a position to offer for her."

"I dare say her trustees would be satisfied if you had a property of your own that could be put into the settlements."

"Very likely. But I haven't any property to settle."

"How would you like to live at Spargrove, Harriet?" asked Richard. "The house needs a great deal doing to it, but it could be made very comfortable with a certain amount of rebuilding."

"Spargrove!" exclaimed Harriet, remembering the beautiful grey ghost of a house, waiting for the right owners to call it back to life. "Oh yes, I should rather live there than anywhere."

"Look here, Richard," said Verney, "you can't start giving away pieces of the estate—"

"Spargrove has never been part of the Wardley estate; the house is no use to me, and it doesn't matter which of us owns the land, provided it is properly managed. I have been meaning to give you a farm in any case, so you can't object if I throw in the house as a wedding present."

Verney still felt obliged to argue, but the two young women saw that the matter had already been decided, and Julia said to Harriet: "You will be able to have the prettiest enclosed garden inside those yew hedges. May I drive over continually and give you advice?"

"Yes, of course. We shall be delighted."

"Will you? I can see that you are going to be my favourite sister-in-law."

"Your sister-in-law! I never thought of that!"

"And Louisa's too," said Julia in a lowered voice. "How is she today?"

"She was still asleep when I came out. I am afraid she is very unhappy."

"Poor woman," said Julia, with a complete absence of rancour. Harriet wondered how much she too had guessed.

She was aware of an unspoken sympathy between

herself and Julia, and of a strong tide of gratitude on Julia's side; there would eventually be a great deal of talking and discussing, which would be made much easier now that she was engaged to Richard's brother—but this was not the moment for confidences.

They had reached the upper end of the lake. The Cascade came flashing over the dark, contorted rocks once more in a single spire of spray; the Grotto, with its flight of steps and crevice window, was no longer in danger of becoming the centrepiece of a Horrid Mystery.

Julia asked Harriet to come back to the Hall with them for a light luncheon, but she said she must return to the Parsonage. She thought she might be needed.

Verney offered to walk back there with her. "I hope they were not offended," she said to him a few minutes later. "Your brother and Julia—at my refusing to go up to the Hall, when they have both been so kind."

"Offended? Good God, no! Couldn't you see them admiring your sense of duty, and thinking what an excellent wife I am going to have."

Nothing in Harriet's previous experience had prepared her for the idea of being valued and appreciated as a member of a family.

She said: "There is something very disagreeable I ought to mention, though I think you must have noticed it already. My—my mother does not love me. And though my grandparents have always given me a home, they never truly loved or wanted me either." And to her own intense disgust she dissolved into tears.

"My darling, don't cry," said Verney, holding her with a fierce tenderness. "The past is over and done with; you shan't ever be lonely again, I promise. From now on you are going to be so loved and wanted that you will not be able to call your soul your own."

They strolled along in a state of unreasoning bliss, but when they got to the drive she said he must leave her, she could not take him into the Parsonage. If they went in together they would give themselves away, and it would be too cruel to parade their happiness in front of Theo and Louisa.

"That's all very well, but when am I going to see you again?"

"Perhaps if you were to walk down after dinner and call on the Rector, we might both by then be a little more composed."

So they exchanged vows of eternal fidelity to carry them through six hours of separation, and Harriet watched him set off between the trees with his long, easy stride.

As she turned away, she caught sight of Chloe coming out of the churchyard.

"What were you doing there?" she demanded, not very pleased to find they might have been observed.

"I was putting flowers on my Mama's grave," said Chloe, with a mawkish expression. "And I saw you kissing my uncle. Are you going to marry him?"

Harriet hesitated. "Yes, I am. But it's still a secret; you mustn't tell anyone."

"Wild horses won't drag it from me," said Chloe earnestly. She gazed in open curiosity at Harriet who, from being quite an ordinary young lady, was about to be gloriously transformed into a bride and, incidentally, her aunt. "You've sat like Patience on a monument, haven't you? And now you're going to marry your true love at last. How lucky you are to be so romantic!"

Why, thought Harriet she is seeing me in the way I have always seen Julia. How very extraordinary.

She stood in the drive, swinging her bonnet by the strings and breathing in the mellow, golden air. Her heart was dancing with delight. Verney loved her. They were going to be married and live in that beautiful house at Spargrove. And as an absurd addition to so much happiness, there was actually someone in the world (even if it was only Chloe) who thought she was romantic.

Her cup was full.

There are a lot more
where this one came from!

ORDER your FREE catalog of ACE paperbacks here. We have hundreds of inexpensive
books where this one came from priced from
75¢ to $2.50. Now you can read all the books
you have always wanted to at tremendous
savings. Order your *free* catalog of ACE
paperbacks now.

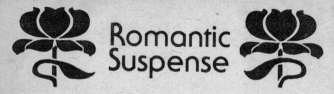

Romantic Suspense

Anne Maybury
Gothics

☐ **Falcon's Shadow**   22583-7 $2.25
The search for her true parents leads a young woman into a
dangerous past.

☐ **Green Fire**   30284-X $2.25
The mysterious Orient held the terrifying secret of the "Green Fire."

☐ **The House Of Fand**   34408-9 $2.25
A young bride finds herself on a terrifying honeymoon of danger
and deceit!

☐ **I Am Gabriella!**   35834-9 $2.25
Karen meets her long-lost cousin. only to have her vanish
again—and reappear with a new identity!

☐ **Shadow Of A Stranger**   76024-4 $2.25
Tess senses that her husband is becoming a stranger to her. Then
one day she overhears the words that are to change her life . . . . if
she lives long enough!

☐ **Someone Waiting**   77474-1 $2.25
A joyous reunion turns into a terrifying nightmare of evil
—and murder.

Available wherever paperbacks are sold or use this coupon.

78c